Red Poppies

by

Lynette Rees

Disclaimer

The historical detail in this book is accurate regarding training for female doctors, treatments by notable physicians of the time, hospitals, battle zones, dates, political movements of the time such as the Suffragettes and 'The White Feather Movement' etc., however, the characters and the actual story itself is a work of fiction. Any resemblance to any real names mentioned in this story are purely coincidental.

ACKNOWLEDGEMENTS

Many thanks Sallyann, for your proofreading skills.

Your help and support with this series of books has proved invaluable!

Thanks to Thea Hartley for her title suggestion. It was a good one to keep in line with the other books in the 'Seasons of Change' series!

'Blowing Free'

A red poppy bows its head
As rows of crosses mark the dead
They gave their lives for liberty
To set men, women and children free

A red poppy blowing free
Marks a spot overseas
In Flanders fields the poppies grow
Where once brave men fought the foe

They left their homes for their country
Bravely going for you and me
Leaving wives, mothers, fathers, sons,
Daughters, friends and little ones

Some returned, scarred by battle,
Treated like prodded cattle
Some fell beneath the dirt
Where those behind felt the hurt

Joyful reunions and happy 'hellos'

To those that returned from the throes

The Great War was to end it all,

But it became a bloody thrall.

Those marked men who got away

Did dearly with their emotions pay

It wasn't the shrapnel that made them blind

It was the horrors that warped their mind

It took a savage loss of life,

To cut the people like a knife

The sun still rises and will still set,

And we free men must not forget...

Lynette Rees 2016

~ DEDICATION ~

This book is dedicated to the men, women and children, who lost their lives in the First World War, otherwise known as The Great War.

Chapter One

September 1916

Adele Owen stood at the graveside and wept bitter tears, but it was not the person who was being laid to rest she grieved for, she'd had a good, long life, but the fallen soldiers she'd encountered in her career as a nurse at the Merthyr General Hospital. The person being laid to rest this afternoon was her Great Aunt Lily from Abercanaid. Her mother Rebecca, was as close to her aunt as her own daughter Mollie had been.

Adele laid a hand on her mother's shoulder. Her mother turned and smiled. "Yes, I know Adele, it's time to depart..." She tossed a white rose into the grave so it fell upon the oak coffin with its gleaming brass nameplate, white roses had always been Kathleen's favourite bloom. And as they gazed down into the freshly dug grave, Adele realised what an impression her aunt had left behind on the villagers of Abercanaid. The large turnout being testament to that.

In the distance, people could be seen leaving the small graveyard, heads lowered, carefully navigating the small pathway as a sea of black, heading back to the chapel for refreshment and a chance to remember the life of Lily Davies, formerly Jenkin, the minister's wife who had once opened a small school in the village. Uncle Evan, the minister, had passed on a few years since and now there was a new minister and his wife ensconced at the chapel.

Adele had been brought up in London, her parents wed there and both had worked at the same hospital, St. Barts: Rebecca Owen as a ward sister and Mansell Owen as a well-respected physician of the day.

Adele vaguely remembered her childhood of boat trips down the Thames and walks through large leafy parks, which had bandstands and lakes; browsing in swank stores in the city as she clung on to her mother's hand; the hustle and bustle of the horse-drawn carriages and omnibuses, electric trams, motor cars and carts as they clattered on by. The hawkers and beggars of the day setting up their pitches on the grimy streets thronged with the masses, as they queued up at penny bazaar stalls, often stopping to buy Italian ice-cream from a vendor, or sitting on a chair to have their shoes shined. She could still see it all in her mind's eye.

Much of her early childhood memory was a blur though because her parents had decided to return to their native town of Merthyr Tydfil when she was just ten-years-old. Her half brothers and sisters being a good few years older than she, remaining in London, now married with families of their own, and she worried about them so living in the big city during wartime.

One night at the end of May 1915, a single German Zeppelin airship appeared over north London and began dropping its deadly cargo on the darkened streets below. This was the first time that the capital had been bombed from the air, Adele hadn't even realised such things could ever happen. The first death she'd heard of via her brother Tommy, was of a young child, a little girl, aged just three-years-old, who'd burnt to death in a fire in Stoke Newington after a Zeppelin had bombed the area. The father of the house managed to rescue his four children from the flames but in the confusion, thought his neighbour had taken his daughter to safety, but her charred remains were later discovered. Tragically, even their eleven-year-old daughter who had been rescued, died some days later. Adele had wept bitter tears of sadness when she heard the news, to think of the suffering of such young children, all in the name of a war being fought overseas.

Adele's father, the eminent Doctor Mansell Owen, shook his head sadly and announced, "This should be the war to end all wars. Germany and Austria-Hungary took a gamble that went badly wrong. 1914 saw a premeditated war of combat and conquest. It's a conflict they thought would be sorted out by now, but instead, it's taken a savage loss of life."

Evan and Lily's only son, Joshua Thomas Davies, was killed overseas, on the first day of the Battle of the Somme in 1916. That day had seen a tremendous amount of casualties, 60,000 in all, of whom 20,000 had died.

"I swear that's what killed Aunt Lily in the end..." Her mother said, breaking into her thoughts. His mother's eyes took on a deep sadness when she spoke. "She was ill and never got over Joshua's death. Those two years he was in the army put pay to her health. It wasn't worth him taking the King's Shilling to lose his life like that. In that respect, I wish he'd been working in the pit or ironworks, he might have lived a lot longer and not had to go to war in the first place."

"You can't tell that at all, my dear," her father said sagely. "He might well have died underground in an explosion or got badly burnt at the works."

Adele had to confess that was true, in her job as a nurse she'd seen lots of accidents from both. She'd enjoyed following in her mother's footsteps, but she now had higher aspirations. She yearned to be a doctor. How was she going to tell her parents this, though? She slipped past them to join her grandparents, Kathleen and Dafydd Jenkin, who'd been speaking to Lily's daughter, Mollie. Mollie smiled at Adele but then was led over to converse with some other mourners from the funeral. There would be time for a chat with her later, for now, she was needed as she was the only thing left of her dear mother.

Adele did love her grandparents so, they were both elderly now but her granddad, Dafydd, still had a twinkle in his eye and her grandma, Kathleen, still sang around the home, particularly when she was happy. But today wasn't a joyful occasion for either of them. Grampa had lost his sister, who he was so close to, and Grandma was fighting to hold back the tears. Adele got in between the pair of them, linking arms. "Come on you two, let's return to the chapel for a cup of tea, it's getting cold out here."

They both smiled and nodded. Adele realised that the person who would understand her need to train as a doctor would be her grandmother. She'd heard all about her stories of going to London and appearing on the stage against her Grampa's wishes, but eventually, he'd supported her dream. She was so proud of her family, she just hoped they would be proud of her too.

***

Following in her mother's footsteps by nursing at the Merthyr General Hospital had its compensations for Adele, it was near enough for her to walk home from work, or sometimes her father sent his driver with the new car for her, but today she needed the walk back to Abercanaid to work out her thoughts. She knew she'd receive opposition from almost everyone for wanting to become a doctor. Yet, she realised she had an extensive knowledge of medical matters that was going to waste. She'd spent hours poring over her father's medical textbooks over the years and questioning the doctors at the hospital about certain procedures, in fact, she felt sometimes she knew more than some of the junior doctors did when they arrived at the hospital.

Many of whom were relieved that she knew so much and could relate her knowledge to them.

After arriving home and sitting down to dinner, Adele cleared her throat and spoke. "I thought I might train to be a doctor!" she announced. There, she'd said it and now her proclamation was left hanging in the air.

Her father turned, and her mother smiled as if she didn't quite believe her ears.

"Pardon?" her father's eyes widened.

"Yes, you did both hear correctly. I'd like to train to be a doctor." She lifted her chin in a determined fashion.

"But that's preposterous!" Her father said, setting down his knife and fork beside his half eaten meal of braised liver, onions, and potatoes. "It's no job for a woman, they've even tried to stop female doctors going to the Western Front before now."

Adele raised her voice a notch. "Yes, I know all about that, but what about that female, let me think now what's her name, she was in all the newspapers a year or two ago..."

"The British nurse, Edith Cavell, was a true war heroine. Is it her you mean?" Her mother chipped in. "She was executed by the Germans after helping hundreds of soldiers of the Allied Forces to escape from the Belgian Hospital she ran in the Netherlands..."

"No, no, I mean a female doctor. I remember now, Doctor Elsie Inglis, she founded her own medical college. She faced a hard time when she offered to take women's medical units to the Western Front. She set up The Scottish Women's Hospital Unit..."

"Yes, I know of her..." her father intervened. "The War Office didn't like her offer to work near The Front Lines and said they didn't want any 'hysterical women' there! Between me and you, I think they didn't want her poking her nose in as her main sponsor was the 'National Union of Women's Suffrage Societies', an organisation with a leaning towards pacifism."

Adele moved in closer across the table to make her point. "But what about Mabel Stobart, Father?"

"The suffragette?"

"Yes, she founded a hospital in Belgium staffed exclusively by women and moved later back to the Balkans to resume hospital work there. And Doctor Inglis, took her hospital units first to France in 1915 and then Serbia, she did some sterling work. You have to admit that?"

Her father nodded then cleared his throat. "True enough, though she was briefly held captive at one point by the enemy, I wouldn't want something like that for my daughter, who knows what could happen. This war was supposed to be over quite quickly and it's been two years and not over yet..."

"Women like Doctor Inglis and Edith Cavell, they are to be admired though and demonstrate Britain's deep involvement in helping her allies?" Adele persisted.

Her father frowned. "Maybe so, but the doctor could have been killed and Edith Cavell was executed by German firing squad, as well you know!"

Adele's chin jutted out in defiance. "Well if you won't allow me to train as a doctor, then I am going to join the nurses at The Front and you can't stop me!"

Her mother smiled nervously, "Please calm down, Adele. You're a fine nurse and needed at the General Hospital. I, for one, wouldn't like to think of you serving overseas. Please reconsider..."

"Look..." said her father, "let's eat our dinner before it goes cold. I admire your passion, young lady. It's highly commendable. I just want you to think it all through."

"I have, Father. I've thought of nothing else this past couple of months since Uncle Joshua died. I want to do something meaningful with my life."

"Is that what you want to do? Become a captive? So you can become a heroine like, Dr Inglis? Or a martyr even like, Nurse Edith Cavell?"

"No! I just want to serve my country somehow!" There, she'd said it and her eyes were beginning to fill with tears and she stood, her knuckles placed firmly on the table. "I want to become a doctor!" she said, her lower lip trembling as she made her point, "or if they do not wish to have me as a physician, then as a nurse...serving at The Front!"

"Very well, Adele. Please sit down," her father smiled. "I don't wish a daughter of mine to go to a war zone, so I think you are going to become a doctor after all and hopefully by the time you are trained up, the war shall be over and done with."

***

And so it was arranged that Adele should commence her medical training at the London (Royal Free Hospital) School of Medicine for Women. The female students were vastly outnumbered by the men she

11

encountered during her training, but it was the biggest opportunity of her life. This school of medicine for women had been founded in 1874 by an inspiring group of women, led by Sophia Jex-Blake, who was renowned for being one of Britain's first female doctors.

Training at the hospital wasn't easy for women as the men often put the women down, it was a man's world but Adele believed she was as good as, if not better than many of those. Although some would have known her father as a well-respected physician back in the day, he had written several papers and researched into Epidemiology, she chose not to tell the other students, she wanted to prove herself to herself first of all and to her male peers, second.

She was booked into digs a short distance from the hospital, sharing a room with a stocky young woman called, Moira. Moira was as feisty as her short cropped hair was red, intelligent to a fault. They often discussed their studies of the day well into the night. Moira though was not as ladylike as Adele, choosing to cuss and smoke herbal cigarettes in a long-stemmed cigarette holder. In some ways she was rather masculine, which Adele found unusual, nevertheless, she was quite fond of the girl.

One day when Adele was well into her first year of training at the hospital, she and Moira were invited to a party at the rooms of Hubert Tavistock, also a medical student. Hubert was a dashing young man who wore bold coloured cravats, and seemed to think of himself as being very Bohemian and free-spirited, which Adele thought seemed strange to wish to become a doctor but remain somewhat unbound by convention. When she and Moira strolled up to the door, they found it ajar, a strange odour drifting toward them.

Adele and Moira looked at one another in amazement. Moira nodded, "Opium!" she said, tapping the side of her nose.

Adele immediately turned on her heel, "Sorry, I'm not going to be a party to this at all," she protested.

"Oh don't be such a pleb, dear!" Moira said grabbing her arm and turning her around to face the front door once more, she grinned wickedly. "It is a party after all, what did you think we were all going to do? Play snakes and ladders?" She giggled.

Hubert appeared at the door, well dressed as usual and his cravat even more garish than normal, his hair slightly messed up. "Come on inside, ladies," he sniffed, his eyes huge and glassy.

Adele had a bad feeling about this as she tentatively walked down the long dark corridor to the back room where the smell was emerging from.

There, lying on a chaise lounge, were two men with a partly clad lady in between them, sharing an opium pipe. Adele froze but Moira pushed her into the room.

A couple of the men stood, one or two she recognised from the hospital who nodded at her, but most of them she'd never clapped eyes on before in her life, which made her feel somewhat unnerved as they looked her up and down.

"Would you like a drink, ladies?" Hubert offered.

Adele's mouth was dry. "Yes, please could I have a glass of lemonade or water?"

Hubert immediately guffawed, looking around the room at everyone. In the corner, a gramophone was playing some unrecognisable song, but it had stopped at that point as everyone stood and stared, somehow making more of the moment than there already was.

"A glass of lemonade or water?" The woman on the chaise lounge giggled and the man beside her massaged her breast over her low cut bodice, the man on the other side followed suit, causing cat calls from the other men. Although Adele had seen plenty of the human body, both when she worked as a nurse and now as a student doctor, she had never witnessed such behaviour before. Even though the woman was nicely dressed, she was in her underwear after all, although her body wasn't fully on view, Adele thought everyone's behaviour was abhorrent.

When all the laughter had died down, Hubert grabbed two large carafes from the table, "I've only got sherry or whisky!" he announced, "there is a war on you know hahaha!"

Everyone in the room laughed, except for Adele herself, she wasn't a big lover of alcohol but accepted a sherry, vowing she would make that last, she didn't intend making a fool of herself. How he could make a joke like that about the war, it rankled her to think of her poor uncle lying out in France, it had been days until his body had been found, and now he was buried in a foreign land. Yet, these young men training to be doctors had come from privileged backgrounds. They appeared very spoilt to her.

"What will you have, Mozzie?" Hubert asked. It appeared to be his nickname for Moira, Adele had not realised until now they were so

13

friendly with one another.

"A whisky of course!" Moira said, rubbing her hands with glee.

"See good old Mozzie here," one of the other men said, "she's one of us! One of the boys!"

He winked at the woman on the chaise lounge, who hadn't seen him as her eyes were rolling back in their sockets as the men continued to play around with her.

Adele shuddered. What did they mean that Moira was one of them? She had no idea.

She and Moira sat sipping their drinks on a sofa near the window, while the men told tales of gawdy operations and new procedures they'd recently observed, whilst poking fun at the female doctors at the hospital. Yet, for all of that, they seemed to respect Moira. She stood up to them and gave as good as she got. She picked up her drink and knocked it back over her head and was immediately offered another.

Moira dug Adele with her elbow. "For goodness sake, lighten up Adele, it's a party, drink that up and have another."

"Yes, and the medical student was skipping with the patient's intestines like they were a line of sausages!" One of the men laughed.

What beastly blokes they were. All middle class with no manners, she'd seen poor people in Merthyr, who had little to live on behave better than this lot. She needed a drink or two to cope with their behaviour.

Before too long, Adele had downed several glasses of sherry and she felt the room spinning around her, she badly needed to lie down.

She was being lifted off her feet and dragged by two people out of the room, down a corridor and into a bedroom where she was put to lie down. She heard several whispers, but was relieved she could have some peace at last as she heard the door click shut, but then she felt someone crawl into bed beside her, saying "Sssh!"

But it wasn't just one person, it was two, someone had got in the other side of the bed. She fought to open her eyes, and could see Hubert one side and Moira the other. Hubert's eyes had taken on a lustful look and Moira was beginning to undress herself. What was going on here? Her head was spinning and everything was going out of focus.

"Sssh now, Adele," she was saying, "you'll like this. We've both fancied you for some time and dreamt of this moment we could both have you. You're such a beautiful woman..."

"A beautiful woman..." Hubert parroted.

Moira was naked as she kneeled on the bed bringing her lips close to Adele's as she felt Hubert's hands roaming up her skirts tearing at her drawers.

Fear had frozen her to the spot, but then something came over her and she roughly pushed Moira away though Hubert was too strong for her, and he pushed her back down on the bed, pinioning down her arms above her head, his hot breath on her face.

"All female medical students get this treatment, Adele!" he sneered, his voice thick with lust.

As she focused and watched Moira's face breaking into a smile, she realised they'd been planning this all along.

Someone screamed a high-pitched, desperate scream, causing Hubert to stop what he was doing and Moira to flinch. It was then she realised it was she herself who had screamed, it seemed to be out of her control as if she were listening to someone else. Her body convulsed as she fought to push both of them away. There was the sound of footsteps and two of Hubert's friends appeared at the door grinning.

"Can we join the party too?" One of them laughed slipping down his bracers over his shirt. "Come on Fred, we'll hold her down so Hubert and Moira can have their bit of fun and we'll have her afterwards..."

"No!" Adele shouted now, but fear was rendering her voice as weak.

The door opened fully and a male voice bellowed, "What on earth is going on here, leave that poor woman alone at once!"

Chapter Two

"Get out the lot of you!" The man bellowed, pointing to the door. In some respects, he appeared as old as her father and seemed to have some sort of authority over the badly behaved crowd as they began mooching away from the room, headed towards the front door.

Adele tried to pull herself up on her haunches but her head was swimming and she flopped back down on the bed, gasping. What had just happened here? Her head was muzzy.

"Not you dear, you remain where you are." The man advised in a gentle tone. "It was obvious what was going on here, I heard your screams and came as quickly as I could." Turning to Hubert, he barked, "Tavistock, I don't want you on my property anymore. Pack your bags now and get out and take all your disgusting friends with you!"

Hubert lumbered up off the bed, muttering under his breath, whilst Adele hazarded a glance at Moria, who was putting her clothes back on. She just shrugged and followed Hubert out of the door along with the other young men who were mumbling, probably annoyed at having the party split up.

"Now stay where you are dear, I'll fetch you a glass of water," the man said kindly.

"Please, Sir, I'd rather get out of this room, I keep seeing what they tried to do to me!" The memory was coming back full force now, the alcohol having numbed her senses. By now Adele was shivering, her teeth chattering and she wasn't sure if it was from the cold or fear. Maybe it was a little of both.

The man, who she noticed was very distinguished looking, extended a hand to help her off the bed. He was quite tall and muscular looking. His dark hair curled and glossy with thin slivers of silver grey threaded through it, and his beard and moustache were well-trimmed.

"Please, Sir, who are you? And thank you for coming to my assistance," she managed to say. Her head was throbbing and she longed for her bed but dreaded going back to her digs as Moira might be there.

"I'm sorry," he smiled, settling himself on the bed beside her. "I'm Oliver Worthington. I own this house and rent out rooms to the young medics, but some of them are disgraceful the way they treat the place. They're an ill-mannered bunch that's why I check the premises regularly. That lot were particularly bad. I called around when I did as the housekeeper put in a complaint about them, I was about to have a word with them but realised something dreadful was occurring. Come this way, they won't be troubling you again. I can assure you of that."

She secured her clothing and he helped her off the bed, then led her down a corridor and into a small kitchen, where he ran a tap and give her a glass of water. "Sip it slowly," he advised. "Please sit down."

She took a seat at the small table and he followed suit opposite. "Now please tell me what exactly happened there?"

Adele took a sip of water. "Moira, the woman who just left, said we were invited to a party, we room together up the road you see, never had a problem with her before. Anyhow, when we arrived I could smell something strange and Moira said it was opium. I wanted to leave there and then but she persuaded me to come inside. There were two men and a woman smoking it from a pipe in the other room. The woman was very indecent..."

"I've no doubt she was a working girl," Oliver explained. "I'm so glad I got rid of them, I don't want any opium pipe smokers in my house!"

"A working girl?"

"Yes, a lady of the night, nymph of the pave, prostitute!" he laughed.

"Oh, I hadn't realised. I mean I've seen them in Merthyr Tydfil. I used to work at the hospital there as a nurse—sometimes they'd show up for treatment when they'd been knocked around by a pimp or a punter, but you could always tell by their garish sense of dress what they were, but that woman was in silks and satins. I thought maybe she was a show girl or something like that."

"Matters not dear, in this neck of the woods, there are some high-class women who could under a certain light, pass as ladies. So how did you know there was something odd about her?"

"She was partially undressed and very free and easy with her favours." She was feeling cold now and rubbed her upper arms to keep warm.

Oliver removed his jacket and draped it around her shoulders, which she was grateful for, then he smiled. "I know the sort. But what I want to know is what happened to you?"

"I was given a glass of sherry, I only wanted a glass of water really but was made to feel awkward and silly for not joining in with the drinking, so I did, but one glass led to another, and come to think of it..."

"What?"

"Moira seemed to be refilling my glass and egging me on, now I know why?"

"What happened then?"

"I was taken to the bedroom, I thought it was to lie down, but it became evident when she and Hubert got on top of the bed beside me what was about to happen. Sir, I've never had carnal knowledge in my life, I wanted to keep it for marriage!"

He nodded sympathetically, then stroked his moustache as if in deep thought. "I can well imagine. You'll have to put all this behind you, and I'll be reporting their raucous behaviour to their superiors at the hospital. I have all their names except for the young lad with the red hair."

Adele would have laughed had her situation not been so dire. "That wasn't a male, it was a female. That was Moira."

"Oh?" he raised a brow. "I assumed..."

"She is very manly for a young lady, granted. But I don't know how I'm ever going to face any of them again." She put her hand to her face and swallowed a lump in her throat as her eyes filled up with tears.

"Now, now, you don't need to fret. I have some sway over at the hospital," Oliver said, reaching across the table and patting her hand.

She wondered for a moment if he were some sort of businessman or political figure to have such jurisdiction, but she felt it might be rude to ask him. "But the problem is that Moira, that young lady, if one can call her that, shares a room with me at a house down the road. I've had no problem with her up until now..."

"What's your name?" He gazed at her intently.

"Adele. Adele Owen, Sir."

"Miss Owen, Adele...you mustn't get upset over these persons, you have done no wrong, from what I can tell of the situation, this has been planned."

She stiffened. "Planned? Surely not?" Her blood turned to ice as she felt her heart might cease pumping at any given time.

"It's the oldest trick in the book. My guess is it was some form of initiation ceremony for you, which your friend, Moira, was part of.

You see a lot of these young male medics hate to think that a woman can make it in a man's world. They see themselves as superior, it's a way of pulling you down a notch or two. You are one of the new student doctors, aren't you? Not a nurse?"

She nodded. "Yes, it's always been my dream to train as a doctor."

"It's my guess..." he carried on, "they might not have gone as far as actually physically harming you, but they would have got you into a position of humiliation. Maybe undressed you on the bed and then called all their friends in to see. To make it appear as if you were of loose virtue."

Adele felt a rush of blood to her cheeks, making her feel hot. She took a few sips of water. "That's terrible. So it must have happened to other female doctors too?"

"Oh, I'm convinced of it. Have any young women training with you, left their position recently?"

"Now, you come to mention it, there were two other young women that Moira had befriended and both of those left for home. One during the first month, making out doctor training wasn't for her, the other a few weeks later saying she was needed at home." It began to make Adele feel so angry she'd been treated that way. "Well I won't be going home!" she said, her lips pursed in a thin line, chin jutting out in defiance.

"That's the spirit, don't let them grind you down, young lady. Now when you've finished your glass of water, I'm escorting you back home to your digs and shall have a word with that landlady of yours about getting rid of her awful tenant, so you shall have the room to yourself for a while. Don't worry, I shan't say a word about what happened here."

Adele breathed a sigh of relief, although she was the injured party, she knew the grief idle gossip could cause, her grandmother had told her that often enough. The legend of Maggie Shanklin still lived on.

Oliver Worthington was as good as his word as he escorted Adele back to her room. He was a perfect gentleman, ensuring she walked on the inside of the pavement and carefully seeing her across the road as the carriages and a few cars, clattered on by.

When they arrived at the room, Adele was relieved to see that Moira had already left in a hurry, all the clothes in the wardrobe had disappeared and several empty dresser drawers remained open.

"Looks like we don't need to tell the landlady about her behaviour, she's gone," Adele said thankfully.

"Tell the landlady what?" Adele turned swiftly to see Mrs Gibson stood behind her, with hands on hips. She was a portly woman with coarse brown hair which was pinned up in a bun, her weather-beaten skin ingrained with wrinkles, but her bright sapphire blue eyes showed how alert and attentive she was. She removed her hands from her hips and placed one hand over the other as she waited for a reply.

"Hello, Madame," Oliver said politely. "Miss Owen has had a recent problem with Moira and we thought it fit to tell you we no longer believe her to be a suitable tenant for you, but it appears she vacated the premises in rather a hurry."

Mrs Gibson's eyes widened. "She's what? She owes me a full month's rent, why that dirty little scoundrel!" She held up a fist of indignation.

"Not to worry," said Oliver, pouring oil on troubled waters, "I shall pay her rent and she can owe it to me."

The woman relaxed her stance and smiled, and then as if realisation dawned said, "But I'm not going to be able to acquire another tenant overnight now to replace her, am I?"

"Of course not, and I shall add an extra few days rent until you find someone!"

The woman looked pleased with that as Oliver extracted some money from a leather wallet from the inside top pocket of his woollen coat. Adele watched as he dropped several sovereigns in the woman's outstretched hand, which she immediately placed in her pinafore pocket.

"Now Adele and I shall be dining out tonight, so you won't mind if she returns at a late hour, will you?"

The woman beamed. "Certainly not, Mr. Worthington, it's quite all right."

Who was this gentleman? Even her landlady seemed to know him?

Mystified, Adele watched as the landlady left the room humming softly to herself as though she had captured the crown jewels themselves in her pinafore pocket, not just a few spare sovereigns.

"Just w...w...who are you, Mr. Worthington?" Adele stammered.

"I'm a surgeon at the Royal Free Hospital, Miss Owen," he beamed.

"But I've never encountered you there before?"

"No, you wouldn't have. I used to work at Barts Hospital, I've only recently taken on a position there."

"But my landlady seems to know you?"

He just smiled and said, "I'll nip back home, now you put your best Sunday dress on and I'll arrive with my carriage to take you to dinner. I'll be back in one hour's time..."

And he left her there standing by the door. A few minutes later, as she was sorting out what to wear for such an occasion, there was a tap at the door.

Hoping it wasn't Moira returning as she'd forgotten something, she tentatively called out, "Come in!"

The door opened and Mrs Gibson stood there, her eyes shining like the sun's reflection on a crystal blue sea. "My dear, how did you get involved with Mr. Worthington?" She blinked several times. Breathy with excitement she relayed, "He's only the most eminent surgeon in the whole of London. He's often in the newspapers. I didn't recognise him at first until he popped those sovereigns into my hand. The man can do wrong in my book, he's a hero! He specialises in some kind of stomach surgery."

"Abdominal?" Adele offered.

"Yes that's the one, I couldn't remember the name, it doesn't exactly trip off the tongue does it, dear? Though you're used to those sorts of terms as you're training to be a doctor, I've no doubt. Anyhow, Mr. Worthington is said to have assisted Doctor Frederick Treves, who specialised in abdominal surgery, he was a fashionable surgeon of the times. He even performed some sort of appendix surgery on King Edward!"

"An appendectomy?"

"Yes, that's the one, another hard word to say! Anyhow..." she carried on in hushed tones, "Frederick Treves was a surgeon for our good King and a couple of weeks before his coronation, the King-to-be became unwell with stomach pains. At first he didn't listen about having surgery, but in the end, he allowed Treves to operate. Whilst he didn't have his appendix removed, Treves drained a lot of pus and badness out of it. The papers said he saved the King's life by removing the poison from his system! Well anyhow, your Mr. Worthington was friendly with the surgeon who performed that life-saving operation. Now you might not be aware of this but Mr. Treves is famous too for helping the Elephant Man, John Merrick! I know for a fact Mr. Worthington was involved in all that stuff too."

"Oh!" Adele hadn't expected that. She wondered just how old Oliver Worthington was if he'd been in the business for so long. Everyone had heard the stories about The Elephant Man.

The landlady nudged her elbow. "Mr. Worthington would be a fine catch for you, dear. He's never married."

"Mrs Gibson," Adele said firmly, "I'm not looking for a husband, my career is more important to me at this point. I shall treat Mr. Worthington as a colleague, that's all. My superior and someone to look up to. But I have to say what you told me is absolutely fascinating!"

"Very well, dear, I understand," Mrs Gibson beamed, "but don't let a golden opportunity go to waste!" she winked, leaving Adele bemused by the woman's behaviour. Why on earth did most women think the answer to everything was to have a husband?

Chapter Three

Oliver arrived to pick up Adele, promptly one hour later. He greeted her by the door of the house, attired in black evening suit, crisp white shirt, cravat and white scarf. He looked every inch the gentleman. She trembled inside wondering just what his designs upon her were. No doubt she'd find out quite soon enough.

She'd chosen to wear a navy shimmering satin gown that she'd only worn once before to a dinner the first week she'd arrived at the hospital. There'd been a special ball held for all the students and it was where she'd first encountered Moira and she'd discovered she would be rooming with her. She dreaded going into class the following day and having to face her once again after what had occurred, and the male students for that matter, but for tonight, she realised she needed to be in the moment.

Around her neck she wore a fur stole her mother had given her, apparently it had once belonged to her grandmother. She loved wearing it as it made her feel so luxurious. To top it all off, she wore long white evening gloves and her hair was piled up on her head, with loose tendrils framing her face.

"My dear, you do look lovely!" Oliver enthused as he took her hand and helped her down the steps and to the awaiting, gleaming carriage outside.

The driver helped her up the steps of the carriage and Oliver joined her, seated opposite.

"Where are we going, might I ask?" Adele enquired.

"It's a little restaurant in a quiet secluded area. The waiters are mainly French and so are the chefs, so we shall be well fed." He rubbed his stomach as if in appreciation.

She hadn't tasted anything French before and wondered about the men at the restaurant being so far from home when there was a war on, although France was one of the allied countries, she guessed they must be fearful for their families' welfare back home.

The carriage made off at a fair speed along the road and Adele gazed out the window at the people passing by in the street, each with their own tale to tell.

"So, how are you feeling this evening, Adele?" Oliver asked, as he twiddled his thin moustache.

"Much better than when you found me earlier, thank you. I feel more composed now. It's frightful when you think I had a lucky escape. I do so feel for those other two medical students who left earlier in the year, probably due to Moira and her male friends' horrendous behaviour. They must have felt so humiliated."

Oliver straightened in his seat. "Most definitely and we shall be reporting all of this, there needs to be some sort of inquiry as to what those young men and that lady did, if you can call her that, it was appalling. It shall not happen again, believe me."

Adele trusted him, of that there was no doubt. "But what will you do?"

"Tomorrow I shall speak to the powers that be and I expect you will be called in to give your testimony at some point."

Adele's forehead creased into a frown. She didn't relish the idea of speaking about personal matters with strangers. "I just don't know if I have the courage to speak out, Mr. Worthington," she said, in all honesty.

"Of course you must, or it will happen again to some other poor, unsuspecting young woman."

She supposed Oliver was right. No matter what people thought of her, she had to stand up for the others, deciding to put the whole thing out of her mind for the rest of the evening, she changed the subject. "Yes, you are right of course, I shall speak out about the matter. My landlady mentioned to me something about you meeting John Merrick?"

He smiled. "The Elephant Man. Yes. It was many moons ago. I was a young protégé back then for the surgeon, Frederick Treves. You've heard of him?"

"Only in passing..." She sat forward in her seat with interest. She had read a little about Treves in medical books with regards to The Elephant Man, but hadn't realised his importance to the King.

"Well, I was allowed to attend and assist at the first ever appendectomy; it was ground breaking at the time as Treves maintained that removal of the appendix was often the only way to go with regards to certain abdominal pains. He wrote a paper about it. Later Frederick Treves was appointed Surgeon Extraordinary to the Queen. He's a remarkable fellow indeed. Anyhow, he'd a couple of years previously, told me about John Merrick, who at the time was somewhat of an oddity, he was misshapen and had been performing at certain freak shows. Then it was pointed out to Treves that John Merrick had been posing in a draper's window opposite the London Hospital we both worked at back then. Frederick had him brought to the hospital for examination and I happened to be there at the time. John, or Joseph as was The Elephant Man's real name, was scrutinised thoroughly by the medics of the day, and photographs taken. Frederick did wonders with Mr. Merrick and they began to regard one another as friends."

"Dr Treves sounds a remarkable man."

"Oh, he is, undoubtedly. He's even performed surgery on the king. Successfully, I might add."

"Mrs Gibson mentioned that."

"Yes, it was in all the newspapers, but you would have been a mere infant back then. Unfortunately as you probably know, he was unable to save John Merrick. Frederick realised he was on borrowed time and helped to improve his final days. He died aged just twenty-seven-years-old."

"So sad."

"Yes, it is, but we mustn't make this evening into a sad occasion. Mr. Merrick's final days on this earth were much happier as a result of his association with Doctor Treves. I highly commend the good doctor for that, The Elephant Man as he was known, came to be treated as one of the human race at long last..."

***

The restaurant was very grand but not that large inside. It was far more opulent than any she'd visited in Merthyr Tydfil. It was embellished with fancy crystal chandeliers and beautiful paintings in ornate frames. A waiter took her stole and Mr. Worthington's hat, cane and overcoat, and another led them to a table in a little alcove. The area was dimly lit, but several flickering candles illuminated the darkness. Adele noticed a beautiful aroma of food cooking coming from somewhere. Once they were seated by the waiter and handed a menu each, she gazed around in awe.

"I bet you're wondering where that lovely smell is coming from?" Oliver asked.

She nodded. "Yes, I was."

"Well actually here, as it's a French restaurant, they cook much of the food at the table."

"Pardon?" Adele blinked several times in astonishment.

"Yes, they fry various flambé dishes such as steaks and Crepe Suzette at the table."

"Forgive me for asking, but what exactly is flambé cooking?"

"It's a sort of gourmet dish where they set fire to the food." Adele had never heard of such a way of cooking before. At home, the food was quite plain, roast dinners, stews, baked puddings and such. "In the case of the Crepe Suzette...they add a little brandy to the orange pancakes and set it alight, a little like someone would do to a Christmas pudding."

"Oh, I understand then..." So flambé cooking wasn't as mysterious as she thought it would be.

"Madame, Monsieur?" Another waiter appeared at the table. "What would you like to order?"

Adele assumed he had arrived to take their food order but it became apparent when Oliver answered that he was a wine waiter, with a small white cloth draped over his arm.

"I think we'll have a bottle of your finest red Bordeaux and a carafe of iced-water, *si'l vous plait*."

Adele was impressed Oliver could speak French. "Is that all right with you, Adele?" he asked, leaning towards her. Might I order for you, too?"

She had no idea what to choose from the menu, so was delighted he chose for her as he jabbered away in French to the waiter.

When the waiter had departed, he said, "I've chosen two fillet steaks with all the trimmings, mushrooms, garden peas and Dauphinoise potatoes with cream."

She had no idea what sort of potatoes those were but was prepared to try them. The chef, in his high white hat, prepared the steaks at the table and she was asked how she liked hers cooked. She had no idea what the chef meant with his flamboyant French descriptions, so followed suit with Oliver's choice of 'medium rare'. Afterwards, they both had the Crepe Suzette pancakes and Adele watched with interest as the pan was lit and went up with a flash of fire which soon calmed down again as the flame died away. She had to admit it was the best meal she'd ever tasted and the wine had been superb, warming her to the core.

"So, my dear," Oliver said, as the waiter went to fetch them a cup of coffee each, "are you feeling any better now?"

"I am indeed and I'd like to thank you so much for bringing me here this evening, and of course for rescuing me earlier."

He smiled a smile that lit up his blue eyes with merriment. "I hope this will be one of many times we spend together."

Something fluttered inside the pit of Adele's stomach, and shyly she looked away. She liked the doctor well enough but didn't know if she wished to be courted by him. It had not been her plan to try to find a husband, her career was important to her right now.

As if reading her mind, Oliver chuckled, "Oh I can see I have you worried, Adele. Believe me, I am not the Big Bad Wolf. I just enjoy your company and ask for no more than that. I have been a bachelor for far too long."

Relief flooded through her. "I am so grateful to you."

"And I to you for your very good company and I expect nor more, nor less, than we shall become good friends."

"I think I'd like that," she said relaxing as the waiter brought their coffee to the table.

***

When Adele woke the following morning for a moment she thought she was back at home as she had her own bedroom but looking around sadly at Moira's empty bed, gave her a sick, desolate feeling in the pit of her stomach. Not only was she now alone in the room but she might end up alone in the classroom and on the wards too, if everyone turned against her.

She got washed and dressed and went downstairs for breakfast where Mrs Gibson had laid the table and left her with steaming pot of tea and several rounds of toast. Unfortunately, although she had enjoyed a hearty meal with Oliver last night, this morning she could barely eat a thing, having to force down a few mouthfuls of toast, though fortunately she was able to drink the tea.

"Did something disagree with you last night, Adele?" Mrs Gibson asked.

"No, it was a wonderful meal, honestly. Mr. Worthington took me to a French restaurant."

"Oh very La de da!" Mrs Gibson said playfully. "Look dearie, if you like I'll cut you a couple of rounds of bread and cheese for you to take with you in case you become a little peckish later on. You need to keep your strength up!"

"There's no need honestly," Adele held up a vertical palm of deference. But her protests fell on deaf ears, as before she left the house, wrapped up warmly for her stroll to the hospital, Mrs Gibson placed a small wicker basket in her hands.

She removed the covering cloth, "There are slices of bread and cheese like I mentioned, a nice rosy red apple, and a slice of my fruit cake!" She declared. Those sovereigns had done a lot for Mrs Gibson's good mood but Adele did appreciate the gesture.

"Thank you, Mrs Gibson. That's so kind of you!"

Mrs Gibson just smiled. "Now on your way, you don't want to be tardy this morning following your late night dining out with the good doctor!" She winked at Adele, causing her to blush profusely.

Closing the door behind her, Adele looked up and down the street, now she was alone she feared that Moira, Hubert and the others, might be lying in wait for her as they realised they might be in big trouble. However, she had nothing to worry about as she walked down the street in the direction of the hospital, the sun was shining, the sky a cerulean blue, and everyone she passed appeared to be in a good mood.

When she arrived at the lecture room, the students were already seated, waiting for that morning's lecture from Doctor Thomas Woodrow-Smythe. It was entitled, 'Respiratory Diseases and Modern Methods of Treatment'. The lecturer had not yet arrived, so the room was echoing and noisy, she looked around but could see neither Hubert nor Moira, and tensed up.

"What's wrong with you?" Belinda the student beside her asked. "You look as though you've seen a ghost?"

"Oh, nothing really," she lied. "Have you seen Moira or Hubert this morning?"

The young woman shook her head. "No, maybe they're unwell."

Though, of course, Adele realised this wasn't the case. Maybe they'd decided to lie low for a few days, that's what it was. It had to be. No one was taking any notice of her and if it wasn't for her thudding heart-beat, clammy palms and slight tremor of her voice, she would feel at ease, but something was up she just felt it in her system.

A side door opened and the doctor stood on the podium to speak, "Good morning all. In the Victorian age," Doctor Woodrow-Smythe began, "respiratory treatments relied heavily on a 'change of air' for patients, such as sending someone to the seaside for example, together with emetic and laxative purgation and bleeding by cup or leech to clear 'impurities' from the body. Medication was limited and the power of prayer heavily relied on back then!"

He paused as the students laughed.

"Diseases such as consumption, otherwise known as Pulmonary Tuberculosis, were endemic, whereas others such as cholera, were epidemic. The coal miners in the pits of Wales are known to suffer from bronchitis, in a chronic mode and other lung conditions too of a severe nature, even pneumoconiosis has been discovered in a pit pony's lung, an example of which I shall show you all later..." Adele glanced across at the various bell jars on a desk behind the doctor as Belinda nudged her in the side with her elbow.

"That looks horrible!" she whispered. Adele wondered why she'd decided to become a doctor in the first place if she was so disgusted by everything, she'd even had to leave the room when they'd watched a recent amputation. It wasn't that Adele herself had a particularly strong constitution, but her nursing experience had stood her in good stead.

"Of course in places like here in London, and other towns and cities where there are factories, sulphurous fogs known as pea-soupers prevail, which can cause respiratory problems. And of course it's particularly bad in match factories as women have been known to succumb to phossy jaw from the white phosphorous in the matches, the phosphorus is also known to cause scarring to the lungs..." the doctor continued.

"My gran told me about that," Adele whispered behind her hand to Belinda. "When she appeared on stage in London, she had a friend who worked at home for the match factory, she told her all about it."

Belinda nodded, then yawned. Adele found it all so fascinating but it appeared to go over Belinda's head.

Quite suddenly, the door opened and to Adele's astonishment, Oliver stood there. He beckoned the doctor over.

"My apologies, everyone!" Doctor Woodrow-Smythe said, "Excuse me for one moment..."

After chatting to Oliver Worthington for a couple of moments, Doctor Woodrow-Smythe returned to the class and facing them said, "There shall be a short recess of twenty minutes which will give you the opportunity to take some refreshment in the canteen." Removing his watch which was on a long chain from his top pocket, he studied it carefully, "That means I shall expect you back at the classroom at twenty minutes past ten o'clock, sharp! I shall be locking this room, so feel free to leave your workbooks and valuables behind when you leave."

Mystified, everyone looked around at one another and there was a loud 'thrum' as people intonated their puzzlement.

"Well, we'd better leave for that cup of tea, let's go quickly so we can beat the others to the canteen," Belinda said.

Adele nodded. They walked down the steps of the lecture theatre and as Adele was about to leave a step or so behind Belinda, Doctor Woodrow-Smythe called her to one side. "Not you, Miss Owen," he whispered.

"Oh?" She watched as Belinda departed with everyone else down the corridor oblivious to the fact that Adele wasn't following behind her.

He gazed around to ensure no one was listening, but the medical students were leaving and chatting to one another, they probably thought the doctor was discussing the lecture with her. "Doctor Worthington has informed me you are to go immediately to his office, where a couple of people are waiting to talk to you about a matter that happened yesterday. Doctor Worthington has filled me in on the details, but I tell you now, Miss Owen, Hubert Tavistock is a fine student who is doing well with his training, I should hate it if he were forced to leave the hospital over a little bit of horseplay!"

Adele felt her hackles rise. "It was not horseplay as you so delicately put it, it was far more serious than you're making out!"

The doctor smiled in such a way that it did not reach his eyes, almost in a threatening manner. "Of course, his father is an eminent surgeon and a valid member of this hospital board so it would be most foolhardy of you to bring his son's reputation into disrepute. Do you understand me? It could mean the loss of your own position here as male doctors are more valid than female ones. Do you follow what I'm saying to you, Miss Owen?" He stared directly into her eyes with that small grin still plastered on his face, unnerving her. It reminded her a little of how a large cat stared at its prey and then devoured it.

"Yes, I follow what you're saying perfectly. In other words, shut up or ship out, Miss Owen!" She turned on her heel and marched out of the lecture theatre as hot tears of indignation welled up in her eyes.

She walked off down the corridor and made her to way to find Doctor Worthington's office, deciding not to inform Belinda, there would be too many questions asked of her.

Locating his room by the brass plaque that bore his name, she knocked tentatively on his door. "Enter!" he shouted.

She was quite breathless, her heart pounding by the time she arrived, and when she saw a woman and a man sitting at a desk beside him, her mouth dried up.

"Please sit down, Miss Owen," he said in a kindly fashion. "This is Mrs Fletcher and Doctor Granger from the hospital board. They'll be sitting in whilst you give them an account of what went on yesterday. I've filled them in on some of the details already, they just need to hear it from you. Mr. Tavistock and Miss Howarth are being spoken to elsewhere at the hospital."

"Hello," she responded to the board members who nodded politely.

She found it a painful process going through what had happened yesterday and worried in case it sounded foolhardy putting herself in that position in the first place. However, she decided to dismiss Woodrow-Smythe's suggestion of not mentioning Tavistock's bad behaviour. What he had done, what both had done, was wrong, and it could happen to some other unsuspecting female doctor sometime in the future if she did not put a stop to it right now.

The lady took notes whilst the other doctor nodded sympathetically, though both said very little, which made her wonder what they were thinking. Half way through, a tray of coffee and biscuits was brought in by a young nurse, which comforted Adele somewhat. She couldn't eat the biscuits as there was a lump of anxiety in her throat, but she welcomed the warm, rich cup of coffee.

Over half an hour later, she emerged from the room knowing she would be late going back to the lecture theatre which would draw attention to herself, added to that fact was that Woodrow-Smythe might question her as his loyalties obviously were with Hubert Tavistock and his father. There was a clock in the corridor and she realised even though she was interested in the lecture, there was only half an hour remaining and she could catch up on it by reading Belinda's notes, so she went out into the hospital grounds, found a bench and ate some of the food Mrs Gibson had provided for her.

Although Doctor Worthington had been so kind to her, she had a bad feeling about reporting the incident.

Chapter Four

Adele was just packing up her basket to return inside the hospital when Belinda called out, "So, that's where you got to? I thought you were joining me for a cup of tea in the canteen and when you didn't return to the lecture theatre, I thought something might be up."

Adele smiled nervously, should she trust Belinda with the truth? Eventually, she said, "Please be seated beside me Belinda, I have something to confide in you, but you must swear to me you will not repeat a word?"

Belinda sat and made a cross sign across her chest. "Cross my heart and hope to die...well, what happened?"

Adele related the full tale of yesterday's events and told her what had occurred at the meeting with the hospital board.

"So, do you think Hubert and Moira will be made to leave the hospital?" She asked, her eyes widening. "Personally, I think they should go, their behaviour was abhorrent."

"I'm not too sure, but I think they were the cause of Jennifer and Matilda's departure from this hospital, earlier this year. I think the ladies were too embarrassed to report them, though."

Belinda twisted a strand of hair around her index finger. "To be honest, I think I would be too, especially as Hubert's father is so prominent at this hospital. And who would have believed them anyhow?"

"Doctor Woodrow-Smythe knows about what happened to me and warned me off earlier but I've defied him. It has to be done Belinda, I have to speak out. No more young women should have to suffer this. Some of the men here are pompous asses!"

Belinda giggled. "Well, you're braver than I am. So, I suppose you're looking for someone else to share your room?"

Adele nodded. "Yes, but it might take a couple of weeks to find someone suitable and what if we don't get on?"

"Well, if that's the case, would I do?" She asked expectantly.

"Oh, yes please!" Adele could hardly keep the excitement out of her voice. "You'd do very nicely and you're much more ladylike than Moira ever was."

"Well that's settled then, I'll come to your digs this evening and ask your landlady if I'm suitable and if she agrees to my boarding with you, I'll give notice on my room, I hate living there anyhow."

Belinda was living in a similar three-storey, large-fronted house across the street, but her house appeared to be not as well maintained, and Adele guessed she didn't have such a nice landlady as Mrs Gibson.

"We should be having our Easter break soon," Adele stood and hooked the wicker basket over her arm. "Will you be going back home to the country, Belinda?"

"I very much doubt it. Father is still overseas fighting the Hun, Mother has turned the house into a temporary hospital for the recovering war wounded. I could go back and help out I suppose, but I'd prefer to remain here. And you?"

"I had thought of returning home, but as it's only for a few days, if you're staying so shall I." What Adele didn't tell her friend was that Doctor Worthington had invited her over to his house over the Easter holiday, she wondered if she dare ask if Belinda could come too. It wasn't that she distrusted the man or anything like that, more that she wasn't quite sure how to behave around him. Whether it was a friendship or something that would eventually develop into much more, but for now, she was pleased to be busy with her new career. Her mother, after all, had married a much older man, so her parents could hardly say anything about that.

"Penny for them?" Belinda asked, as they made their way back to the hospital.

Adele shrugged. "Oh, I'm not really sure they're worth that much."

"Go on, I'll wager they are. I bet it's some lad or other you're mooning about. Say, is it, Humphrey Longhurst? Or Benjamin Parkes? Or..." Belinda named a few medical students in their year.

"No definitely none of those." Adele smiled to herself, wondering if Belinda would believe her if she told her who she had designs on, she guessed she wouldn't.

***

That afternoon they were led on a ward round with the medical team where they visited patients with various heart and respiratory conditions. The wards were long and narrow in a nightingale style with the ward sister's desk being in the middle of the ward. Metal framed beds were lined up against the walls, military fashion. The place had a strong smell of carbolic and disinfectant about it that could only be attributed to a medical establishment.

"So, does anyone have any idea what this patient is diagnosed with?" The consultant, Doctor Browning asked the large group of medical students. He was referring to a middle-aged man who was well propped up with pillows, the man's lips looked quite blue and his breaths seemed rapid and shallow. Browning had an air of arrogance about him, appearing to look down his long, aquiline nose at the group. He was a tall, fair-haired man, who Adele guessed came from good stock.

No one answered, and Adele could sense the doctor's impatience as he tapped his foot, arms folded as if he was counting down the seconds of a clock to get an answer from someone. Even though she thought she might know the answer as she had come across something similar during her nurse training, she was reluctant to reply in case anyone thought her a know-it-all.

"Come on, come on!" he barked in an impatient manner. "Cough, shortness of breath, slight fever, fatigue, the expectoration of thick sputum which is quite often green! Would that be a heart condition or respiratory one?"

Of course, they all knew the answer to that one—it was a respiratory disease.

"Right, now can someone be more specific as to which condition exactly it might be?"

The Doctor gazed at the group of male medical students as if expecting them to answer, totally blanking the few female students present.

Adele cleared her throat. "Chronic Bronchitis, Sir!"

Doctor Browning narrowed his eyes as if he couldn't believe a woman would get the answer before one of the men, as slowly he turned in her direction. "That is correct!" he exclaimed, then making eye contact with her, he continued. "And what are the causes of Chronic Bronchitis?"

"Well, it can be caused by environmental factors, Sir...air pollution and dust. I know of several coal miners who had the condition often in conjunction with emphysema. They were also smokers of pipes or cigarettes, which might have precipitated the disease."

A big smile appeared on the doctor's face. "Splendid, young lady! Now, what is your name?"

"Adele, Adele Owen, Sir."

"Adele, I have a feeling you are going to be an asset to this hospital. I take it you have some experience of medical matters?"

The consultant's question put Adele in a difficult position, she hadn't wanted to show the others she had once worked as a nurse but thought maybe honesty was the best policy. "Yes, Sir, I began training as a nurse in Merthyr Tydfil in South Wales, which of course is a large industrial town where we have both the ironworks and coal mines to contend with."

The Doctor drummed his fingers on his chin as if deep in thought. "Hmmm I bet you could teach this lot a thing or two," he laughed. But Adele hadn't wanted the doctor to draw attention to herself. One or two of the male students glared at her and she noticed a couple of the females whispering to one another. Her cheeks began to burn, then thankfully, Doctor Browning led them on to the next patient. This time, she had no clue what the condition was and neither did any of the other medical students. Apparently the lady who had a saddle-shaped nose was born to a mother who had a sexual disease. "This lady," the doctor informed them, "has Congenital Syphilis..." Adele felt desperately sorry for the lady and was about to approach her to speak to her when one of the male students, Adam Samuels, said, "Perhaps you'd be better off in the sluice room with the bedpans, Nurse Owen, rather than attending to medical and surgical matters." His male colleagues guffawed at his put down, but the female students looked around sympathetically toward her plight.

"That's quite enough of that," Doctor Browning scolded the young man. "Miss Owen appears to have far more medical knowledge than any of you lot have. Her nursing experience has stood her in good stead."

Adam lowered his head and muttered something under his breath. Oh dear, at this rate she was going to gain lots of enemies and lose the few friends she already had.

After carrying on with the ward round without incident, it was time to head home for the day. Relieved, Adele let out a long breath, realising worse was to come when she had to finally face Hubert and Moira.

Chapter Five

The same evening, Belinda had sorted things out with both landladies and moved into Adele's room. Her own landlady was not happy about it of course, but Belinda paid up all she owed and she left the house with Adele in attendance, helping to carry her bags. The landlady, Mrs Walters, sniffed, "Yes, see if you'll get such good accommodation with Mrs High and Mighty Gibson over the road there. You'll be back young lady, with your tail between your legs!"

"Take no notice," Adele said, "she's probably jealous as Mrs Gibson has a lovely house and very high standards."

"That's true, Mrs Walters hardly ever as much as flicked a duster around her parlour or living room..."

By the time Belinda had settled into Mrs Gibson's lodging house and they were just about to settle down to supper, the landlady had made them some boiled kippers with bread and butter, when there was a knock at the front door.

"Who on earth can that be at this time of an evening?" Edna Gibson rose, a haughty look on her face. "It better not be Mrs Walters or I'll give her all the way to go...I will," she said, turning to look at the two young women.

Adele heard a man's voice in the hallway and then the sound of the voice getting nearer, Mrs Gibson was bringing him into the parlour. Adele stiffened, "What if it's Hubert Tavistock or his father?" she whispered to Belinda. But as soon as she saw who it was she ran to greet him. It was her half brother, Thomas.

"Thought I'd come to surprise you," he said softly, and then she was in his arms as he hugged his sister tightly.

He winced slightly and she apologised. "I'm so sorry Thomas I was forgetting."

He smiled and drew away, "I don't..."

"How could you, but you manage so well!"

Mystified, Belinda and Mrs Gibson looked at the pair. "It's all right both, it's my leg, it's partly wooden," Thomas tried to make light of it. "Was blown off in Ypres, Belgium, but at least I'm lucky...the rest of me made it home."

There was an awkward silence and then Mrs Gibson broke it by asking, "Would you like to dine with us, Mr. Owen?"

Thomas removed his hat and nodded eagerly. "I have to admit I am famished, I've travelled across London and there was a little walking involved, but it's worth it to see my baby sister."

"Then sit you down," Mrs Gibson said brightly, as she went off to dish up more food, returning later with a large kipper and some more bread and butter.

As the four were seated at the table, they all tucked in and chatted easily with one another. It was so good to see Thomas once again. After they'd eaten, Belinda asked Thomas questions about the war.

"I was involved in the second battle of Ypres..." he explained. "The Hun used a poisonous gas which killed many, but I was fortunate I got away with that."

"What happened to your leg then?" She pressed as Mrs Gibson gave her a stern glance.

"Shrapnel. It was removed by an army doctor but got infected, so I was shipped back home. No doubt I'd still be there otherwise."

Belinda looked utterly absorbed in what Adele's brother had to say, but then her hypnotic state was rudely interrupted as Mrs Gibson said in her best posh voice, "That's quite enough now, Belinda. I'll be serving the apple pie and custard soon and we'll have no more talk about the war!"

Belinda sighed but Thomas just winked at her, causing Adele to think that maybe her brother secretly liked the attention.

At the end of the evening, Thomas said he was going to look for a hotel for the night but Mrs Gibson insisted on giving him a bed to sleep in. One of her lodgers had gone back to their family for the Easter holidays. Thomas offered her money for his board and lodge, but she was having none of it.

"It's brave men like you that are laying their lives down on the line for our freedom, it's the least I can do." Mrs Gibson smiled.

***

The following day, Belinda and Adele set off for the hospital, leaving Thomas in Mrs Gibson's capable hands, who told him after she'd finished her morning duties, she was taking him to see the memorial gardens in the local park.

As the women arrived at the hospital, Hubert Tavistock was waiting near the main entrance, he had two young men, who as she drew closer, she realised were Adam Samuel and another medical student from the group, with him called, Winston Hamilton.

"I wouldn't bother going in there, *ladies*," Hubert sneered. "Best you go back home today."

"How dare you!" Belinda glared at him. "We are perfectly within our rights to enter the hospital."

"You can enter, Belinda, but not if Adele is with you," Adam said.

"But why ever not?"

Hubert stepped forward, the two young men following suit, as if to intimidate both ladies. "Because today is the day my father and the hospital board will be excommunicating her from this hospital after all the lies she told about me!"

"Lies?" Adele yelled. "They were not lies, now get out of my way!"

Hubert and his two friends stood on the steps with their arms folded. They were all tall men of around six feet or so, whilst she and Belinda were many inches shorter and did not have their physical prowess.

"Very well," Belinda said.

Adele glared at her. "Are you out of your mind? We have to get past them for this morning's lecture."

"Don't worry," Belinda whispered to her friend. "We shall get in." Then linking arms with Adele, they walked away from the hospital entrance and down the road.

"What's going on?" Adele demanded to know.

"It's a hoot really. I know of another way into the hospital via the boiler house at the back, come on, you'll see."

Belinda led her friend to the back of the hospital where there was an open door and a man shovelling coal into a barrow and down a warren of dark, narrow corridors, until they were on the ground floor, then up a wooden staircase and there they were, outside the lecture theatre.

"Good or what?" Belinda laughed.

Adele had to admit it was a great ruse. "But how did you know about it?"

"Sid, who works in the boiler room, showed me this way. I helped him out after he injured his wrist and he said it was handy for me to know, but not to tell anyone about it. Though on this occasion, I'm sure he wouldn't mind at all!"

They sat in the lecture hall waiting for it to fill up, when finally Doctor Woodrow-Smythe stood on the podium about to start as the clock ticked to exactly 9 o'clock. He greeted the class and then went on to talk about the modes of transmission of infection for a few minutes, then quite suddenly, the double doors were thrown open wide as Hubert, Adam and Winstone, burst into the room as everyone stared at them.

"Tavistock and you other two young men, why are you late?" the doctor asked.

"I...er...we...er..." Hubert's face flushed and when he looked up and saw Adele and Belinda giggling at the back of the room, he glared, as if known on this occasion, he was beaten.

They got through the rest of the day without much event, but there was still no sign of Moira, making Adele wonder if the young woman had returned home.

When Adele and Belinda arrived back at their digs, Mrs Gibson was on the doorstep waiting for them, her face pale and ashen, her wrinkles even more engrained than usual.

"What's happened?" Adele asked as she drew near.

Mrs Gibson's hands flew to her face. "Oh, something dreadful happened this afternoon…"

Adele ushered her inside the house, whilst Belinda went off to make some tea.

As they all sat supping the hot, sweet brew, Mrs Gibson related her tale to them, the colour now returning to her cheeks. "Your brother Tom and I had enjoyed a nice morning strolling through the memorial gardens. It was a lovely day, the sky was blue, the sun was shining, we were admiring the flowers and took time out to sit on a bench, as of course due to Tom's infirmity, he needs to rest up once in a while…" she sniffed loudly.

"Yes, go on, Mrs Gibson," Adele prompted, slightly irritated that the woman was taking her time to get to the point.

"Anyhow, as we sat basking in the sun watching children running around and one was even flying his kite, two well-dressed young ladies approached us. At first, I thought they were going to ask us something...you know maybe the time or directions to some place. But the one young lady had something in her hand that she gave to your brother…" She stared at the carpet and slowly shook her head.

"Which was?" Adele asked, feeling she wanted to yell at Mrs Gibson to spit it out.

"A white feather!" she said, now lifting her eyes to meet with

Adele's own.

Belinda gasped laudably, whilst Adele froze in horror, the hairs on the back of her neck bristled.

"Your brother took it very well," Edna Gibson carried on. "Quite the gentleman he was and didn't even tell them he was a war veteran. Meanwhile, I was absolutely livid as you can well imagine. Thomas silenced me as the women stood glaring at him as if to make him nervous of their presence. Then he stood, tipped his hat to them and began to walk away, of course by this time when they could see his bad limp, they realised their very grave error, particularly as his wooden leg made that strange hollow sound on the path. I shouted at them, "Leave this man and others like him alone! You women are causing no end of problems. You caused one sixteen-year-old lad to sign up underage because he was called a coward and told to wear his sister's dress! That lad died out in Flanders the first day he arrived! Are you satisfied now?"

Adele rose from her chair and hugged the woman. "Thank you for that, Mrs Gibson." A tear sprang to her eyes.

"It just wasn't right Adele, your brother is a courageous man and he didn't deserve that kind of treatment. A right gentleman he was about it and all, but you could tell he was humiliated. We had planned on going to the ice cream parlour, but by then it was as if he was like a deflated balloon inside, so we came back here and he went straight to his room for a lie-down and he's still there. Meanwhile, I kept watch on the door to see if those women were still out and about handing out white feathers, but there was no sign of them."

"Hopefully, they might have learned their lesson, especially as you gave them a piece of your mind, Mrs Gibson," Belinda said thoughtfully.

"Well, I hope so," Mrs Gibson folded her hands on her lap in a very prim manner, her lips firmly set.

"I think I'll rouse my brother and bring him in here with us for a cup of tea," Adele suggested.

"And I shall make a fresh pot!" Belinda announced.

"Thank you, dear," Edna replied, "there's a slab of fruit cake in the larder, please cut it up and give Mr. Owen the largest slice."

Belinda beamed. It was obvious Edna was pleased with her new tenant. Later, they all sat amicably around the table, where the 'white feather incident' was not mentioned at all. Tom seemed none the worse for it, but Adele guessed it had happened more than once and she wondered how many other war veterans had to put up with that sort of thing.

***

The following day back at the hospital, Adele was astonished to see Moira in some sort of clandestine conversation with Hubert, they both glared at her and Belinda as they passed them by.

"Wonder where she's staying of late?" Adele asked her friend.

"I wouldn't worry about it—she can have my old room if she wishes at that dark, dingy place opposite, that would be good enough for the likes of her!" Belinda said in a loud voice with the obvious intention of it reaching Moira's ears.

"Sssh!" Adele warned. "I don't wish to antagonise those pair any further, they're in enough hot water as it is!"

As they rounded the corner of the corridor in the direction of the lecture theatre, Dr. Woodrow-Smythe, was waiting at the double doors to ward off the students as they arrived. Several had gathered around. He waited a while, then announced, "There is to be a change of plan this afternoon—you are to observe an operation. Mr. Bellingham is to perform a double amputation on a wounded soldier. The poor man's legs are badly damaged but he got shipped back from France this morning."

"Isn't it strange how surgeons are referred to as 'Mr.'?" Belinda whispered.

"But couldn't that operation have been performed out there?" A male student shouted out.

"Why, yes of course," Woodrow-Smythe replied. "His feet were already amputated and initially, it was thought it was all he would require, but there was a sign of gas gangrene setting in. The young soldier has other problems—it appears he has sugar in his urine. So, what could that indicate?" He asked the group.

"Diabetes. Sir!" Adele answered quickly, without thought. She had seen enough diabetics during her role as a nurse to realise that a condition like that could complicate matters regarding the patient's progress and recovery.

For a moment, she thought Woodrow-Smythe was going to ignore her outburst, but then he replied, "Very good, young lady." Then he quickly changed the subject.

"I wager you if that had been one of the male students, he'd have

41

got a pat on the back and a 'congratulations!' to boot," Belinda said seriously.

"No doubt..." Adele sighed inwardly. There was just too much prejudice against female doctors for her liking. It was a man's world, that much she was sure of.

The operation was interesting to observe, but Adele had to support Belinda, who almost fainted twice at the shock of the amount of blood loss incurred. The odour reminded Adele of a butcher shop she knew in Merthyr Tydfil that had row-upon-row of severed pigs' heads in the window and sheep and cow carcasses strung from metal ceiling hooks inside the establishment. Beneath customers' feet was the scattering of sawdust to absorb the blood. The smell was the same fresh, iron-infused blood that she was smelling right now at this moment. A fresh blood, but this was from a living person. Some young man who had gone off to fight for his country in a yonder field of muck and mayhem. Someone, who had left behind family and friends, and someone who was fortunate. Not fortunate as insomuch as to lose two limbs, but fortunate he still had his life intact. Though what kind of future would there be for him now? To be wheeled around in a chair, helpless from the waist down? The amputation was mid thigh on both legs, so quite high up. He'd need plenty of rehabilitation—that was for sure.

Belinda was swaying by the side of Adele, her face a putrid green.

"Take a few deep breaths in and out!" Adele hissed as she took her friend's arm to support her.

"I think I'll have to go outside for some fresh air…" Belinda groaned.

This was just what Adele did not want to happen. It would be playing into the male students' hands to see such weakness. None of those had to leave the theatre.

"Look, just hang on a few more minutes, then we'll be out of here…"

Belinda nodded, but her face reflected the true colour of how she felt inside.

The surgeon was beginning to suture the final stump before sending the anaesthetised patient to the ward.

"Of course, this young man will require regular nursing observations…" he was saying. "He will be at high risk of infection and must be monitored regularly. He will probably also develop certain sorts of pains. Anyone any idea what sort of pains they might be?"

Adele knew the answer but hesitated from replying so not as to appear to be too clever. But when no answer was forthcoming from the group, and the surgeon appeared to become impatient as Dr. Woodrow-Smythe glared at them all, shaking his head, she cleared her throat to speak.

"Those would be phantom pains, Sir."

"Very good!" Mr. Bellingham replied. "Now what exactly are those?"

"Well...he might wake during the night and feel a pain in what were previously his limbs, reaching out to touch them...though of course, they will not be there any longer. So he might require sedation, Sir."

Mr. Bellingham raised an eyebrow. "And how do you know so much about this, young lady?" He peered over his surgical mask intently at her.

"I have worked with amputees at the hospital where I was originally training to become a nurse."

"So they had the war wounded at that hospital?" He seemed highly interested.

"No, Sir. Several were coal miners who had been involved in pit accidents. Crush injuries and the like."

"And where is this hospital?"

"Merthyr Tydfil, in South Wales, Sir."

He turned away and carried on suturing up the remaining stump of the limb as a nurse in a pristine white, well-starched uniform, presided by the side of him.

So he was unimpressed that she had worked as a nurse in a hospital in a mining community in Wales, that would be it. After all, many of the eminent surgeons and physicians of this London hospital appeared to have a plum in their mouths. She felt like going over to him, tapping him on the shoulder and asking why he had left their conversation mid-flow, when quite suddenly, he turned around on his stool and to her surprise said, "That is very interesting, I would like to discuss this further with you sometime?"

She nodded, as she felt a hot flush creep up her neck and toward her face. Interesting? What she had to say would be interesting to a London surgeon of his ilk? She glanced around at some of the other students who were muttering behind her back.

"Of course, Sir," she replied, sounding more confident than she felt.

"Teacher's pet!" She heard a male voice behind her chant.

"I've heard she's very free with her favours, isn't that right, Tavistock?" Adam Samuel sniped at her.

She turned to see that at least Hubert Tavistock had the good grace to look embarrassed. There was plenty she'd love to have said, but this was neither the time nor the place for it and fortunately, the surgeon was so intent at his job-in-hand that he didn't appear to hear what was going on around him.

To flounce out of the theatre would make her look like a silly female, so instead she said, "If you lot spent more time observing a great man at work and took more due care and attention to your studies, you could all become great men yourselves."

Her remark did the trick of silencing them, and she got some appreciative glances from the women on the floor.

Later that afternoon she was called into Woodrow-Smythe's office, expecting a ticking off as he appeared to be previously taking sides with Hubert Tavistock and his father. She was surprised when he smiled and asked her to be seated.

"Thank you," she said as she sat opposite him, at his large imposing, ornate oak desk.

"It's come to my attention, Miss Owen..." he began, "that you are an exceptional student at this hospital and shall be rather an asset here. I can sense that you are having some ribbing from the male students and that something distasteful happened recently at the lodgings of Hubert Tavistock, but rest assured..." he paused as he steepled his fingers, "whatever happens, whether he gets away with this or not, I shall be putting in a good word for you myself. We cannot afford to lose an excellent student like yourself from this hospital."

She was at a loss for words, she hadn't expected support from the one person she had assumed was against her.

He gazed at her for the longest time, "Well, Miss Owen, what have you to say about the matter?"

"I honestly do not know what to say, Doctor. I'm so used to most of the males being against me at this hospital that your offer of support has come somewhat of a surprise to me!"

He chuckled. "That's understandable, but bear this in mind, I do not stick my neck out for many at this hospital, but when it comes to yourself, you are a brilliant student with a bright future ahead of you, who will jump over the heads of that lot out there!"

"Even Hubert Tavistock?" She raised an eyebrow.

"Even him, but please don't tell his father I told you so. It wouldn't go down well at our gentleman's club if I enthused about a female student over a male one. I had a word with Mr. Worthington and he's spoken to Mr. Bellingham and I think too, you've impressed him today. He told me he'd like to train you up as a surgeon."

She gulped. "Me? A surgeon?"

"Yes, you'll have to finish your training of course, but if you could spare the time on your days off to come in and observe, that would be incredible. Both for yourself and for this hospital."

She drew in a breath of composure, then let it out again. This, she hadn't been expecting.

"I shall have to give it some thought..." she mused.

"What's to think about?"

"It's just I thought I'd complete my training and then decide what to do, which way to branch out as it were."

The doctor paused before speaking, "To be totally honest with you...I think the surgeon is looking to train people up to go to The Front with him. He intends setting up a casualty clearing station there, as there is great need. It shall be arranged by the RAMC, The Royal Army Medical Corps."

"The Front?" She blinked several times. It was something she had admired others for, especially Doctor Elsie Inglis who had set up her own hospital for the war wounded.

"Don't think you got the mettle for it?" Woodrow-Smythe teased.

"I think I could give it a go, yes, but what about my training?"

"My dear," the doctor said, sitting forward in his chair, "what better training could there be for you? Granted you'd be thrown in the deep end, but that's the way to learn!"

"I shall have to give this some serious consideration," she said, all of a sudden feeling extremely shaky indeed. One moment she had entered the lion's den thinking she was to have an extreme ticking off, the next she was being put forward as a surgeon on the Western Front. She'd once thought of going as a nurse there, but never in a million years thought she'd get to work as a doctor out there.

"Well, don't think too long or too hard about it. Mr. Bellingham wants someone to mentor to take with him and he seems very impressed with you."

The problem wasn't what she thought about this herself, but what would her parents say about her going to a war zone?

Chapter Six

Adele deliberated over the proposal all night. She had told Belinda, who tried to dissuade her from going to the Front Line, Mrs Gibson didn't comment at all, just tutted and shook her head. But it was her brother, Tom's reaction, that surprised her the most.

"I think you should go—they are in desperate need of good medical staff out there. When I was injured, you should have seen how many were piled up around me, waiting for surgery. Of course, they had to operate on the most crucial cases of all first, my pain and suffering moved me up the line, and to be honest with you, it made me feel a bit guilty, especially as some men died while waiting for surgery. Go, Adele, the men need you out there."

Her brother's final words that night somehow permeated her senses and by the morning, her decision was made. She would take this brief intensive training with the surgeon and accompany him to the Western Front, after all, she would be assisting him and would not be the main surgeon out there.

**

Adele had asked Oliver if she could take Belinda with her to visit his home on the Easter Monday, it was not that she was afraid to go alone, on the contrary. It was more that she thought about Belinda being lonely during the Easter break.

They arrived at Oliver's large house with some trepidation. Adele's family home back in Merthyr seemed small in comparison even though it was considered the largest in the village of Abercanaid. This house was high-walled and surrounded by trees. The black painted, wrought ironwork gates gave it an imposing appearance. They rang a bell at the gate and a butler appeared, who walked them up to the doorway which had large pillars and fancy stonework steps. It was quite the most elegant house Adele had ever seen. The panelled wooden door was painted black and had a large brass knob in the middle, and a little higher up a matching brass knocker in the shape of a lion's head.

The butler pushed open the door and led them into a hallway that took Adele's breath away. Belinda looked up at the ceiling and then all around, gasping in astonishment at the beautiful marble staircase with its mahogany bannister, and above that a long oval window with leaded glass which let in a lot of light. On the walls, were various pieces of art depicting scenes all over London: The Thames, St. Paul's Cathedral, Big Ben, and then, smaller works of art of a variety of flowers. She had to admit that Oliver had good taste.

The butler took their coats and then showed them into the drawing room, where the fire was lightly ablaze.

They waited awhile, the rhythmic tick of the grandfather clock in the corner, comforting Adele. Then they heard a slight cough as Oliver sauntered into the room, with a big smile on his face.

"Ah, ladies, so good to have you join me!" He enthused. "I hope you don't mind, but I've invited James Bellingham along."

Why should they mind? Adele was going to have to work at close contact with the man soon and it would be nice to see him out of a hospital setting.

A maid served them sherry and canapés as an aperitif while they waited for James to arrive. "I'm so sorry, I'm late, everyone!" He explained when he turned up later. "I was supposed to be on hospital leave but an emergency appendix turned up last minute, I couldn't very well say no. The poor blighter had perforated it and there was a chance the poison would get into the blood. Anyhow, all went well and he's now recovering on the ward."

Adele met his eyes which were the darkest of brown, almost black but so shiny and full of life. She noticed if he was excited about something, they lit up.

They all chatted amicably, James asking her about life in Merthyr Tydfil. He seemed most intrigued by it, as he originated from Oxford and had attended the university there before undertaking his medical training.

What she really loved about him was the way he made her feel so good about herself as if he was really listening, and she had noticed that Belinda hung on to his every word.

They were then led into the dining room, where a vegetable soup and crusty bread was served, followed by a roast beef dinner with Peach Melba for dessert. During dinner, Adele became aware of James catching her eye across the table and she blushed and looked away. Belinda seemed unaware of James's interest toward her friend and she kept chatting away, as James's eyes played games with Adele's.

Oliver seemed more than happy with all the company he had, as he explained it was a large house for one to be rattling around in. On more than one occasion Adele had wondered, why at his age, he had not married. He seemed too good a catch to be a bachelor. Belinda said she imagined he'd once fallen in love with an Italian Contessa and she'd jilted him at the altar, so he was never able to love with such free abandon again.

Adele had laughed realising that her friend had an over active imagination. Still it was such a waste him living alone, that much was evident.

Chapter Seven

Ypres, Belgium September 1917

Adele couldn't believe she was finally here in a makeshift tented hospital in Belgium, where occasional gunfire and the noise of bomb blasts, shook the ground beneath her feet. The third Battle of Ypres was now well underway. James Bellingham, who had given her intensive surgical training of the most basic procedures over the past few months, had finally told her when she had given him the news of her agreement to join him, that he had specifically chosen her not just because she seemed a head and shoulders above the other students, but because she also had previous nursing experience which would prove invaluable. She would be expected to liaise and sometimes take charge of the nursing team too.

The first week there had been hard for her as she spent her days sometimes assessing casualties to see which men needed priority treatment, just as Thomas had told her would happen. It was sometimes a difficult choice to make, but if it came between a life and death decision and an injury that could wait, then life always won the day.

The heat and humidity wore her out that first week, and having to stand and assist Mr. Bellingham with operation after operation, often which required the removal of shrapnel, amputation of body parts, packing deep wounds or even resuscitation on the table, seemed all too much for her. Eventually, she got used to the days no longer being her own. Some days she even forgot to eat, if it hadn't been for the nursing staff bringing her a sandwich and a cup of tea in a tin mug, she would have starved.

It rained often and it got extremely muddy underfoot around the encampment, making conditions even worse than they already were. Ambulances and other vehicles often had to be pushed out of the mud with great difficulty as the men huffed and puffed, swore and groaned, but the determination to get the vehicles going again, never waned. Adele rarely got seven hours of sleep at night as often her rest got disturbed by gunfire or explosions in the distance, or the sounds of vehicles and voices bringing in freshly injured soldiers, interrupted her sleep.

The last person she'd operated on had upset her deeply, the injuries so severe, that there was a hole as big as her fist in his abdomen. Thankfully, he'd passed away, but not before she'd administered an opium-based injection. He'd fallen into a deep sleep with the word, 'Mama' on his lips. She was later to discover—he was just fifteen-years-old. He'd lied about his age when he'd signed up to fight for his country. A lad too young to die, who should have had his life stretching out in front of him. He was someone's son. Someone would receive a telegram to tell of his passing. He would be sorely missed and leave a big hole in the pit of someone's stomach, much bigger than the one that had killed him in the end.

She had to admit, she'd shed more than just a tear that night and fallen onto her bed thoroughly exhausted. The bed itself was little more than a narrow camp bed, with a couple of army blankets to keep her warm, but it was a better condition to sleep in than those who slept on the floor on pallets who were at risk of being woken by rats that often found their way to the encampment. Though the relative few she saw, were nothing compared to the ones the soldiers themselves described in the trenches as being as 'fat as cats'.

She had drifted into a deep sleep of dreams of her homeland and family when she heard a soft female voice beckon her.

"Och, Adele, wake up. We're expecting another few ambulances full of injured men. I've brought ye a cup of tea before they arrive."

For a moment, she thought she was still dreaming, until she opened her eyes and saw Morag, a young Scottish nurse from Dundee, holding out a tin mug of tea in her hand. Adele sat up and took it gratefully from her, it would be many more hours before she'd have the chance of another.

"Thanks so much, you're very thoughtful."

Morag smiled. Even in the dimly lit tent, where there were only a couple of lanterns lit, she could see the young woman's dazzling smile. She was the sort of person who lit up a room with her presence, always positive, forever cheerful, an asset to be around.

Morag sat in a chair sipping her own tea, it would be hard work for her too later. Harder in some respects as she had to run hither and thither, looking for this and that for the medical team, whilst they only had to attend to the task-in-hand.

The nurses, though, sometimes did the doctors' jobs if they were not around and were well-experienced. She knew that herself from the time she'd spent as a nurse back in Merthyr. The ward sister there could diagnose as well as any of the doctors, and more often than not, was correct with her diagnoses.

At first light, the ambulances arrived and the stretcher bearers brought in the casualties to the clearing station. Adele had had hardly any time to draw a breath for the first half hour or so, the large tent was in chaos as the injured were sorted into those requiring immediate surgery and those that could afford to wait. All the other casualties were in another tent. Some could wait, others were already dead by the time of arrival or else on the brink. Often Adele heard one or another of the men cry out with delirium, their limbs shivering, lips trembling. Shell shock, they called it. Some of the poor men would never be the same again. Fortunately, for some, with the right help, support and guidance, they became physically whole again, though they'd never forget the mental anguish, ever.

Worst of all were the firing squads—who on the command of a senior officer would shoot a deserting soldier, as they brought shame on the army and could prove a security risk if they fell into enemy hands. Adele often wondered if those poor men were just shell-shocked and refusing to take any more, their bodies shutting down, their need to escape, their only outlet from a hell on earth. Life in the trenches was arduous. Often they were stuck in inches of wet muck with no means of washing, changing or drying their clothing. Although they were told to change into clean socks and dry their feet, it didn't always happen that way and as a result, many soldiers developed something known as 'trench foot', a painful condition. The constant mud and rain had exacerbated the condition for many. Often the foot would crack and change colour, then swell up as blood vessels and nerves were damaged in the process. If untreated, then gangrene could set in resulting in amputation to save the soldier's life. One soldier arrived at the clearing station and his toes fell away when his socks were removed, the stench being unbearable. Adele had to inform him that his limbs had to be removed as soon as possible.

The sounds and smells they endured as they worked at the encampment was like nothing she'd ever witnessed before. Here, there wasn't much cleaning up of areas, like at the hospital. It was very rough and ready, often a quick sweep and mop of the floor were all they had time for. No time to disinfect operating tables as time was of the essence, a delay could mean the difference between life and death. Often wounds were already infected from mud and manure from the fields, the medical staff were really up against it.

One young man lay on a gurney whimpering in the corner of the tent. There was no time to attend to him. Adele wished she could split herself in two, realising that a lot of her decisions meant the difference between life or death. She was in the midst of suturing a wound when the young lad cried out, "Mam! Where are you?"

Morag left the operating table as Adele was able to manage alone for a while. She knelt beside the gurney and took the lad's hand. He wanted and needed his mother, but she was in a distant land. Adele watched Morag stroke the soldier's head and softly kiss his cheek. A smile appeared on his face, he held out his arms as if he was embracing someone, and then he was gone, in the belief his mother was him. If there'd have been time, Adele would have wept, but there were many more casualties to attend to and she just didn't have the time to spare. No time to ponder her decision on whether she'd have saved the lad if she'd operated on him first. Only God knew the answer to that.

Adele didn't have the time either to dwell on her dry mouth, aching back and limbs, and her growling stomach. Something spurred her on, propelling her to get through the day's work. James Bellingham was beginning to leave more and more cases in her capable hands to work at another hospital over the Belgian border in Northern France. That one was in a large château that had been taken over for the war effort. The men were transported there by ambulance and even trucks after their operations. If then found to be chronically unwell, they were shipped back to Britain, where special hospitals were set up to deal with the aftermath of burns, amputations and shell shock.

At that time, there was also pioneering plastic surgery being carried out at various British hospitals. Some of the men had received horrific burns to their faces and other parts of their bodies, making them barely recognisable to their families and friends.

The first time James had left her alone with the nursing team, she had trembled from top-to-toe, but a professionalism had taken over, along with a comforting word from Morag. After a couple of minutes of adrenaline coursing through her veins, she had calmed down, realising she was doing the best she could under the circumstances. James, who checked out her work when the casualties arrived at the hospital, informed her he was very pleased with her work indeed, which gave Adele an immense feeling of satisfaction.

It wasn't planned that she would head a surgical team but there was little choice as one of the senior surgeons had fallen ill, so it was either in at the deep end or let the men die. There was no other choice.

Apart from a quick cup of tea and a small corned beef sandwich, it was 4.30 p.m. before Adele got to go off duty, when another surgeon, who had rested most of the day, took over for another long shift.

The cost of this war was high and seemed totally futile to Adele.

***

The following day, Adele received a letter delivered by the Red Cross, it was from Doctor Oliver Worthington in London. It read:

My Dearest Adele,

I hope all is well? I do worry about you being so close to the enemy line, but at the same time here have much admiration for the work you are doing at the clearing station, and for your utmost bravery at what must be such a trying time for you.

Things are going well here at the hospital, and I know that even though you have been taken out of your training as it were, you will be learning so much more on the job at Ypres rather than if you were here practising on dummies and other medical students.

I ran into Woodrow-Smythe the other day and he was extolling your virtues. Something I feel I do have to tell you is that Hubert Tavistock and that female friend who used to share a room with you, have been expelled forthwith from the hospital. They were discovered smoking opium at his family home. The dim wit thought his parents weren't due back from their holiday in Scotland for a few more days, so they were caught off guard. The place was turned upside down and ransacked, the servants given a long leave of absence whilst Hubert, his female friend and other non-entities, had a wild party! As you can imagine, his father was livid and has sent him away to stay with relatives. The talk at our gentleman's club is that as Hubert made a mess of his doctor training, he should now be forced to sign up and fight for his country.

Anyhow, you shall hopefully, never have to set sight on either Tavistock or that uncouth young lady [and I used the term lightly], ever again. Tavistock's father has withdrawn his complaint against you. Common sense has prevailed at long last.

Please let me know if you are due to return to Blighty any day soon! I so miss our little chats.

Yours,

Oliver.

Adele reread the letter once more and placed it under her pillow. So Oliver was thinking about her. Hopefully as much as she was thinking about him, when she had the time. The letter was some respite from the arduous days she spent at the encampment.

That night, she slept soundly. It was the best night's sleep she'd had in ages. It wasn't just because Oliver had got in touch with her, but because he'd said she'd never have to face Hubert or Moira again. That thought had overshadowed her thoughts of returning home.

There was talk that maybe this war was coming to an end. It had been going on for three long years, but Adele dismissed it as rumour-mongering—no such luck, she expected. Though people said the arrival of the Americans would hasten the defeat of the German army.

To the North East of Ypres, things weren't going too well. At Passchendaele in October 1917, it did little but rain for the entire month, so that many soldiers went down with trench foot, such were the conditions they had to endure from the cold, rain and mud. It really was a hell on earth for them. The Third battle of Ypres had been launched on the 31st of July, 1917 and continued until the fall of the village of Passchendaele on the 6th of November. Adele prayed for the day when it would all come to an end.

She had become increasingly concerned about Belinda, after discovering she'd joined the Suffragette Movement back home. They were the women, headed by Emmeline Pankhurst, who fought for women's rights. But they were sometimes inclined to violence and only in 1913 had blown up David Lloyd George's house, and all this whilst he was thought to be a supporter of the right of women to vote. It made Adele wonder if they could do that to someone who supported their cause, what would they do to someone who didn't?

Though Belinda had informed Adele in one of her very long letters that Miss Pankhurst had instructed the Suffragettes to stop their campaign of violence and to support the government and its war effort, so that demonstrations were more peaceable, but Adele still remembered the buildings the women had set on fire and the letter bombs. She hoped Belinda would not get herself involved in anything like that.

Adele's thoughts jarred back to the present moment as a man was brought into the tent by two stretcher bearers, shivering and shaking so badly that he almost toppled off it.

"Shell shock!" The bearer, whose name was Arthur, said.

Of course, she'd immediately recognised the condition. "Between me and you," Arthur carried on, "I hope for his sake whilst he's over here he doesn't get discharged as they'll send him straight back out to The Front. Only a few months ago this happened, they got sent to that hospital that takes the overflow from 'ere, and the poor bastard was sent back to his death. He just couldn't take the noise of the explosions."

"Ssh!" Adele warned. "I don't want us to disturb this man's mind any more than it already is."

Arthur nodded. "Sorry, Doctor Owen. It's just it makes me feel so angry." She noticed a tear in his eye and patted his arm.

"I know you are, Arthur. I dislike it myself the way the men get treated, and sometimes it's by their own superiors who should be taking care of them."

He nodded. "Very well, Doc, we'll leave him here. But please try to put some kind of word in for him, send a message to the hospital when he gets there. This man can take no more. His name is Donald by the way."

A lump arose in Adele's throat. How she wished she had the authority to do what she could with the men when they were due for discharge. Even some who had been sent to British hospitals had been despatched back to The Front instead of returning home to the families who loved them. What kind of war was this?

She leant close to the man and whispered in his ear, "Donald, we're going to get you fit and well again, I promise you that."

He shivered uncontrollably as his limbs made sharp jerky movements. "Nurse, a strong sedative, please!" She called out to Morag.

Morag returned a couple of minutes later with an injection which Adele administered to the man, within ten minutes he was asleep and his muscles had ceased jerking.

"This is awful," Adele complained to Morag. "Arthur told me that some of the men are this way due to the trauma of being told to take no prisoners. He explained to me that one young man had to bayonet a couple of German soldiers in the face, and as a result, developed facial tics. It's a psychosomatic thing, almost as if the men take on the injuries of the men they have wounded or killed."

Morag grimaced. "The ones who are going back to Britain, where are they being sent to?"

"Some have been sent to the East Suffolk and Ipswich Hospital. But Mr. Bellingham has told me that a psychiatrist will be at his hospital soon to try a talking cure with the men."

"A talking cure?" Morag furrowed her brow. "Never heard of that before. How can that possibly help?"

"Well, the psychiatrist, Doctor John Bowden, says that it's cathartic for the men to relive traumatic events. Some are having severe nightmares where they wake up screaming and shouting, it's very scary, Mr. Bellingham says it disturbs the whole ward."

"Yes, I can well imagine that happening..."

"Anyhow, Mr. Bellingham says that he'd like me to be involved in this talking cure thing and he'll bring someone here to replace me."

Morag frowned. "Och no. I'd hate to lose you here, Adele. I cannae be thinking of you leaving us all! You're a brilliant surgeon, you've saved so many lives."

"And lost a lot too along the way," she replied sardonically.

"Ye cannae save everyone! What shall I do without you? You understand the nursing staff so well as you were once one of us."

Adele looked her colleague firmly in the eye. "Well, this is what I was going to tell you...Mr. Bellingham has informed me that I can bring one person from the nursing team with me and I've chosen you, if you don't mind?"

Morag's eyes lit up. "Mind? I'm absolutely over the moon! I'm ginna afta give ye a big hug, hen!" She embraced Adele so tightly, she could hardly breathe, but it was nice to see her colleague so happy.

If they could just help one soldier like Donald, it would be something, Adele supposed.

***

The hospital itself was an old mansion in the heart of the French countryside that had been taken over for the war effort. The family were too afraid to remain there as it was so close to The Front Line, so they had fled further inland to stay with relatives but had given permission for the château to be used.

The former ballroom was made into a ward for the men with rows

57

of beds lined up against the walls, and in the middle of the room was a nursing station, comprising of a large wooden table and a couple of chairs. On top of the table was a ledger where the men's records were recorded. Portable curtained screens afforded the men privacy when various medical procedures or nursing care was required.

Another large room was used as an operating theatre and yet another as a treatment room. There was even a rest room for the men which had a wireless radio and some comfortable armchairs, but best of all was the view outside the château with its rolling green fields and wooded areas, it made for a picturesque scene indeed. So the nurses would take the men out there if it was a nice afternoon to enjoy the sun. Some patients walked unaided, some with assistance, some were wheeled out in chairs and others even wheeled out in their beds. But of course, if there was news of a battle close by, then they remained indoors. Thankfully, so far, the hospital had not taken a direct hit.

The medical staff themselves, used the upstairs bedrooms as their quarters, a few nurses shared one room, and three doctors another. Adele and Morag were fortunate to share one smaller room between them. There was an upstairs room which had a bath, but the privy was out of doors. There was one for the staff and one for the soldiers, though many of them needed to use bottles and bedpans if they were incapacitated.

Adele keenly observed the men on her first morning at the hospital, most she didn't recognise as they hadn't stayed long previously at the clearing station, and of course, they didn't recognise her as earlier she had been gowned and masked up as she performed operations and various other procedures. One, she did recognise though, was Donald, as he had only passed through a couple of days previously. She approached his bed, where he was sitting up staring vacantly out of the window.

"He appears to have gone blind," Mr. Bellingham said in a hushed tone.

"That's strange," said Adele. "He could see when he arrived at the clearing station. I clearly remember him looking at me when the sedation had worn off. He told me I had lovely green eyes."

Mr. Bellingham stroked his chin. "And so you do, Adele," he enthused, then his voice took on a grave tone. "This appears to have happened to several men we've had through here. Initially, I thought it was due to the explosions having an impact, but now I'm not so sure of it."

"Whatever do you mean?"

He relaxed his stance. "Well, I have been told that the talking cure sometimes helps. One soldier, who seemed to have severe stomach pains, once he began talking to the psychiatrist and explained that he'd had to push his bayonet into a German soldier's stomach and kill him that way as he was ordered to take absolutely no prisoners by his commanding officer, discovered the stomach pains mysteriously disappeared, almost within a day or so after speaking about it."

"They never returned?"

"No."

She drew in close to him. "So, what are you implying Mr. Bellingham?"

"I'm thinking that his symptoms were psychosomatic as in imaginary."

"Strange you saying that as one of the stretcher bearers told me of something similar the other day. But why do you think that's happening to these men?"

"Guilt, most definitely. The horrors of having to attack and maim another human being and of course take away their lives. They see themselves in the men they kill."

Adele pondered on that thought for a while. "What can I do to help?" she asked.

"John Bowden will be here tomorrow to speak firstly individually with the men. I'd like you to take notes and encourage them to write about their experiences. Then in a few days, he plans on sitting them all down in a circle where they'll discuss what they went through and are going through right now."

"Do you think that's wise though, Mr. Bellingham? I mean the British have always been known to keep a stiff upper lip. Won't their superior officers think they are cowardly to sit and talk about their feelings?"

"Let me deal with that, Miss Owen. Those superiors are too harsh on these men. If I'll have my way they won't be returning to battle. Though we do need to take care as some could be malingering. But we'll soon discover who those men are."

"Malingering?"

"Yes, only last week one of the men who had been diagnosed with shell shock was found to be walking with a 'dancing gait'. He almost pulled that off until one of the nurses followed him outside and when he thought no one could see, he was walking as normally as you and I. When he'd been discovered, he made such a fuss about it, begging us not to tell his commanding officer. We didn't, but we told him we would pretend he had got well again but would have to return to battle. So he got a month away from the fighting and returned there yesterday."

"How will you feel though if he dies?"

"I have thought of that, but the man was taking up a bed of someone who might genuinely be suffering from shell shock, that was the deciding factor for me."

Adele had to agree that Mr. Bellingham had a fair point. "I understand."

"Now, I'll remain here with you for a few days and once you're settled in, I'll be going back to work at the clearing station."

She nodded. At least here at the château, it was a more comfortable environment and although she would still be at work, in a sense she looked on it as being a rest.

"Come on, I'll show you around the operating theatre, treatment rooms, et cetera, then I'll take you on a ward round with the patients notes so you can familiarise yourself with the cases we have here, many of whom of course who will have already passed through the clearing station under your capable hands."

After showing Adele around, so she could familiarise herself with the place, he took her to his office. "There's something I feel I should tell you and you might not like this..."

"Oh?"

"It's Hubert Tavistock, I've heard he's arriving here next week and has been made a captain in the army, it's all down to his upbringing and class of course, some of the army superiors are right 'Hooray Henrys' who have seen little combat, yet are quick to send their men into battle or in front of a firing squad for what they perceive as cowardice."

Adele's stomach lurched. "Well, I hope I shall not have to encounter that beast. He shouldn't have been accepted into the army after that incident with the opium pipe."

Mr. Bellingham cleared his throat. "Yes, I heard all about that and his consequent dismissal as a student doctor from the hospital. Let's hope neither of us has to encounter him. No doubt Daddy, who used to be an M.O. in the army himself, put in a good word for him. Jobs for the boys and all that. His father saw action during the Boer War, but of course is deemed too valuable to send out here. His skills are required at home. Anyhow, I thought I ought to warn you."

"Thank you for that, Mr. Bellingham. I do appreciate you telling me. Now I won't have such a shock if we do encounter one another."

"Now how would you like a cup of coffee? You'll enjoy your time here as the environment is much more relaxed than working at the clearing station. I'll be headed back there shortly, so let's relax while I still can!" He chuckled.

"Thank you, Sir." Adele found it hard to call him James whilst they were at work, even though he'd given her permission. He was still her superior after all.

Refreshment was sent for, and a French Red Cross nurse returned with a tray containing the cups of coffee and a couple of slices of sponge cake. They spent the rest of the afternoon discussing various cases, then Mr. Bellingham took her on a ward round so she could familiarise herself with the patients, who required long-term care.

Later, she returned to the ward alone to speak with Donald, he sat there vacantly, unseeing, in the chair and she guessed he must be sedated to stop the heavy jerking of his limbs. This war had a lot to answer for.

"Mr. Richardson, Donald..." she began.

He turned his head in her direction. "Who is it?"

"I'm Doctor Adele Owen. I treated you at the clearing station a few days ago. Do you remember me?"

"Yes, I do," he said, straightening up.

She drew up a chair to sit beside his bed. "When I first met you, you could see me, you commented on my green eyes. But now I'm told your vision has gone completely?"

He nodded. "I remember speaking with you Doctor, I remember your eyes, but yes, my sight has now gone for good."

"I'm not so sure about that, Donald. We are going to bring a psychiatrist here to speak with the men and try a talking cure. It's thought that your condition could be psychosomatic and that speaking about it could help you."

Immediately he withdrew and began to shake. "No! I can't!" he shouted out as if the very memory of what had happened was too much for him to take.

For a moment, she feared what to do, it was such a shock to his system. "Just calm down Mr. Richardson, no one will force you to do anything you don't want to. Take nice deep breaths."

He followed her instructions and within minutes had calmed himself. This wasn't going to be as easy as she first thought.

***

However the following day, Donald agreed to be seen by Doctor Bowden but only if Adele herself was present, which she agreed to as she wished to observe anyhow. It took Donald some time to get used to talking openly to the doctor and when he became upset, Adele calmed him down, then later Morag sat with him and soothed him.

"I think," Doctor Bowden said, "that as Mr. Bellingham suggests there is no real physical cause for his blindness. This is psychosomatic. He told us he blames himself for the death of a young German soldier. Hopefully over the next few days, he will tell us more."

As Donald began to build up his trust in the medical team, it transpired that when he went to shoot the young officer who was charging right at him, his gun failed to fire and he had to mount a bayonet and stick it between the officer's eyes in his forehead. He said the young man had fallen backwards onto a heap of bodies and stayed there staring at him whilst he removed the bayonet. He said he'd had nightmares over those bright blue eyes that seemed to be looking into his soul, questioning him. Why? Then, within hours, Donald had lost his eyesight.

"So, there's an element of regret here?" She asked Doctor Bowden.

The psychiatrist stroked his chin, "More than an element of it, I'd say regret, guilt and condemnation. Donald hates what he had to do so much that he's subconsciously punishing himself."

"But he was given orders not to take any prisoners, so what else could he do? Allow himself to be killed?"

Doctor Bowden nodded. "Precisely, I know that and you know that, and so does he, though it doesn't help him at all. It's a natural reaction, I'm afraid."

She nodded and then went off to fetch them a cup of tea. Meanwhile, she bumped into Morag who was carrying a silver bedpan to the sluice room.

"How is Donald now?" she asked.

"So, so. He sleeps a lot, which is good and he seems to be shaking less and less but the guilt will just not leave him."

"Sad what those poor men have had to endure," Adele said thoughtfully. "Doctor Bowden has said it might help some of them to write about their experiences, though of course as Donald has been struck blind, it would be difficult for him."

"I could assist him," Morag said brightly. "He could tell me what he wants to write and I could jot it all down. It might help a wee bit."

"Splendid idea!" Adele said. Then she left to fetch that cup of tea for herself and the doctor.

Over the following few days, Morag and Donald built up a rapport with one another, he trusted the young nurse. She took the time to sit and talk with him as things were far less hectic at this hospital compared to the clearing station. Adele noticed how tenderly Morag behaved around the young man and how well he responded to her gentle coaxing. Finally, it was time for all the men to have group therapy with Doctor Bowden, with Adele and Morag in attendance.

The session went well as they all sat around with their chairs in a circle as the doctor had recommended. Adele had never seen anything like it before, but was open to the idea. Some men wept openly in front of their peer group, whereas others were still a little guarded, but as the days went on, all the men opened up one way or another as there was a bond of trust there between them.

Then one day, Donald actually told the group how he'd had to bayonet the young German soldier between his eyes. No one was shocked, there was a murmur of agreement that they would have done the same thing faced with the same situation. If they had allowed him to live, they might have been faced with a court martial and possible execution. There was a strong policy of taking no prisoners and as his ammunition had run out, what other choice did he have?

"I wish..." Donald said, with his head lowered, "it had never come to that but..." he paused.

"But what?" Doctor Bowden asked gently.

"But I had to go with what my head told me and not my heart..." his body shuddered as he was wracked with grief and wept bitter tears of regret.

The other men looked on in sympathy for his plight, many trying not to weep themselves, but Adele noticed a few silent tears amongst them and thought it a good thing as her mother had told her tears were nature's way of healing someone.

Doctor Bowden brought the session to a conclusion and the men who could walk unaided went back to bed, whilst others were assisted by nurses and medical orderlies. Morag escorted Donald to his bed, tucking him in, then after about a quarter of an hour Adele noticed he was fast asleep, which was unusual for him as he often had sleeping difficulties.

A couple of hours later, Morag came running towards her. Fearing something was wrong, Adele said, "What's going on?"

"It's good news!" Morag said, "Donald opened his eyes a few minutes ago. He can see again! His sight has returned!"

Relief flooded Adele's veins and a tear trickled down her cheek. "Go and see if you can find Doctor Bowden," she ordered. "He was outside talking to a patient a while ago."

Morag nodded, her eyes shining brightly.

So Doctor Bowden was on to something with this talking cure, that much she was sure of. He would be an asset to this hospital.

***

Mr. Bellingham had told Adele about Jean-Matin Charcot, a French doctor who became known as 'the Napoleon of the neuroses'. Mr. Bellingham continued. "Charcot used hypnosis on patients, it was previously thought that only women got symptoms of hysteria, but this war has proved it happens to men in combat and in the trenches. That's why Doctor Bowden and myself are pushing this 'talking cure'."

"There's something else that concerns me, Mr. Bellingham," Adele stressed.

"Yes, go on..."

"Well, it's what will happen to these men if they are cured? It has occurred to me that unless they remain here, and I can't see that happening as the beds are badly needed, or shipped back to England, then if we deem them fit, we could be sending them back to a certain death."

Mr. Bellingham stroked his chin. "You are right of course, Miss Owen. It's something that concerns me greatly. I want the men to get well again but of course, if they are fit, they might have to go back to The Front Line. I shall stress to their commanding officers that an adequate period of rehabilitation is needed and that they should return to Britain for recuperation. Hopefully, then maybe this blessed war shall be over and they won't have to see active combat again."

Adele nodded her head sadly. "Yes, we need to delay things for as long as possible, if only this hospital were just for the shell-shocked, traumatised soldiers, but every day we get someone referred here from the clearing station, mainly for care following amputation, trench foot or even a sexual disease. How can some of those married men do that kind of thing to their wives back home, having sex with strangers behind their backs? I'll never understand it."

Mr. Bellingham looked her squarely in the eyes and lifting her chin said, "Because it is wartime, Adele, and these men know they could be on borrowed time, so they look for solace wherever they can find it. Even if they have to pay for it."

A tear trailed down her cheek. Really she did understand it because although she and the doctor were not in the firing line, they were near enough to hear muffled explosions and know that one day they could be killed too. Maybe tomorrow would never come. James held her gaze, and for the first time, she saw the compassion inside him. Up until now he had been very professional and not crossed a line, but now she could see from his smile he was breaking down a barrier between them. Softly, he touched her cheek and drew her to him, kissing her on the lips, then he drew away leaving her heart beating like thunder. He'd stolen her breath away but this was neither the time nor the place.

"James..."

She was about to say something when quickly he said, "Can we meet one another tomorrow afternoon? I know we both have some leave—we could take a picnic. The weather's lovely, just to get away from the hospital would be nice. We could sit in one of the fields near the wooded area and if there is no noise of gunfire we can pretend the war isn't happening for a couple of hours..."

She nodded wanting him to kiss her again, but this was neither the time nor the place.

"I'll give you a knock at about 1 p.m. tomorrow afternoon then. There's plenty of left-overs in the kitchen we can take with us."

"I'd like that..." she said barely in a whisper.

Their intimate moment was broken as Morag knocked on the door and popped her head inside. "Sorry to disturb you both, but one of the men is getting agitated. He says he must get back to the Front Line or people will say he's a coward!" she said, breathlessly.

James Bellingham frowned. "Oh, we can't have that!" he said, "I shall come along at once and have a word with the poor man."

Fortunately, on that particular occasion, the doctor was able to talk the man down, but the number of daily arrivals at the hospital was making it all the more likely that some would have to return to the Front Line.

***

Adele waited for James to arrive the following day, she wore a pretty summer dress that she'd brought with her but hardly had a chance to wear. It was a warm day for the time of year and she wrapped a shawl around her shoulders in case it got chilly later.

She'd waited for about twenty minutes and was about to give up hope, when James burst in through the back door. "I'm sorry Adele, I bet you thought I wasn't coming but I had some work to finish off first, there was a complication after one of this morning's operations and the surgeon who took over from me wasn't as experienced, so I stopped on for a while. The soldier in question is now out of danger!"

"Oh, of course, work and saving men's lives must always come first!" she said, so pleased to see him. He looked so different when he dressed in normal attire. He wore a smart tweed jacket, open-necked shirt with a cravat and twill trousers. Smart but casual. His handsome face broke into a smile.

"I hope you like ham, cheese and crusty bread?" she asked.

"Yes please, I could eat a horse to tell you the truth, I'm so ravenous. I haven't eaten for hours." He rubbed his stomach.

"I've also packed some fresh fruit, there's been a good fall of apples in the grounds." She whipped a cloth from the top of the basket to show him all she'd placed inside. "I've also managed to acquire a couple of slices of fruit cake and a bottle of home-made lemonade!"

"That all sounds divine," he said as he took the basket from her arms and offered his other arm for her to link with him as they left by the back door of the hospital.

As they left the hospital behind and headed for the fields, Adele felt free, although she wasn't really, it was the nearest they would get to it out here in Northern France. Many of the villagers had already left to stay with family elsewhere. It was too dangerous for them to stay, and they both realised they mustn't stray too far for fear of falling into enemy hands. But James reckoned, the farmer's field next door should be all right.

After walking for several minutes, James vaulted over a wooden stile and Adele handed him the basket, then he helped her over and she fell into his arms the other side. He was so close she could feel his warm breath on her face, then he kissed her with a deep passion. A passion he couldn't show in the hospital. Then he stopped to gaze into her eyes.

"Oh Adele, don't you realise how I feel about you?" he asked. The thudding of his heart next to hers, told her his feelings were strong but Oliver was at the back of her mind. Was he waiting for her back in London?

He broke away. "You look troubled?"

"It's not that, James. I do have feelings for you but his war confuses things, let's see how we both feel when we return to England?"

He nodded, vigorously. "Maybe you are right. Let's enjoy the picnic for now and forget all our worries for the next couple of hours. I promise I shall be the perfect gentleman."

And he kept to his word as they talked and laughed, picked wild flowers and spoke about their plans for the future. The time went all too quickly but it was a time of rest and relaxation for both of them, something that they needed so badly. For a couple of hours, it felt as if the war just wasn't happening anymore and Adele wished that really was the case.

***

Doctor Bowden wrote to a colleague back in England and arrangements were made for several of the men who were suffering from shell shock, ones who were making the greatest strides, including Donald Richardson, to be shipped back to another hospital to recuperate. Adele heaved a sigh of relief and so did Morag. Though to Morag, it was a double-edged sword as she was going to miss Donald very much but at least he would have a chance to rest and recover that way.

"Please don't worry, Nurse Morag," Donald had soothed, "after this war is over, I'll find you again some day and I intend to marry you."

Morag had beamed. If this had been some other sort of hospital then relations between a nurse and patient would have been frowned upon, but the war made life all that more precious and provided an immediacy to people's plans. Things they wouldn't otherwise have considered, or at least would have waited for, now they did not.

Donald became very positive and upbeat whilst he waited for news of the soldier shipment to England. So did some of the other patients. That night they were soundly asleep when there was the sound of heavy vehicles and voices outside. It was dark except for the vehicle headlights, then there was a hammering on the double doors, which Adele and Morag went to answer, fearful of what was going on. It was usually so quiet at the hospital during the night.

Adele unlocked the door to find a man in military uniform stood in front of her, flanking him either side, were several other soldiers of lower ranking. "I am Captain Frederick Jennings and I've been given orders to move out some of the malingerers from this hospital and take them from here back to the trenches!" He said.

Adele took a sharp intake of breath and felt the ground was coming up to meet her, she wished James were here right now, he'd have more authority, but he had returned to the clearing station where he was most needed.

"There are no malingerers here!" She said sharply.

"That's not what I've been told. I have orders, so you shall have to point the men out to me who shouldn't be here or I shall be forced to capture them."

By now the patients themselves were stirring and she could hear the noise of mumbles and groans. Then Donald walked towards them.

"Doctor Owen," he said. "It was only a question of time. I realised this thing about us going back to England would never happen."

"But it's already in progress, you are to leave here in a few days," Adele protested. Doctors, Bowden and Bellingham, want you to return to England to recuperate.

Bravely, Donald spoke up. "I've spoken with the men and five of us have agreed to leave, we are the five who were due to go back to England. If we do not return to the trenches, then other men might have to go in our place and some of them here, well they're in a worst state than ourselves."

Adele turned to the captain. "Might I see evidence that you are to remove men from this hospital?" she asked.

He handed her a piece of a paper with the official documentation which had been signed by his superiors.

Adele's chin jutted out in defiance as she stood her ground. "Orders or no orders, you cannot take these men. They cannot go 'over the top' again—it will be too much for them to bear. I am their doctor and I am telling you they have been suffering from shell shock. Donald, here, was struck blind until recently! Please find Mr. Bellingham, the surgeon, at the clearing station and ask him. Or Doctor Bowden, their psychiatrist."

"Forgive me Doctor, but all that psychiatry stuff is a nonsense if you ask me. These men are shirkers and I'm taking them back where they belong. And I do not take any orders from a woman, doctor or otherwise!"

"I bet if Mr. Bellingham was here, you wouldn't come here like this!" It was then it occurred to her that maybe the unit had waited for the surgeon to return to the clearing station before making a move on the men.

The captain put his foot in the door and shouted, "Come on now men, get dressed and come with me, otherwise I shall be forced to arrest this doctor and the nurse as obstructing us in our line of duty and you wouldn't want that now, would you? They could both face a firing squad for refusal to comply with army orders!"

"You bastard!" Adele spat out her words, looking at Captain Jennings, surprising herself with the vehemence in her voice as he and his men forced their way in through the double glass doors.

Donald took Morag's hand as she openly wept. "I'll be back Morag. Don't you worry about me." He removed a sovereign from his pocket. "Keep this to remember me by," he said soberly. "It's my lucky sovereign, it's kept me safe out here, now I want you to have it..."

"I can't take that, you need it more than me," she said, pushing it back into his hand. But he insisted and gave it back to her, it was useless for her to protest, it gave him comfort that she should take it and remember him. She nodded, the tears falling from her eyes, she could speak no more, she was in too much distress.

"Now get a move on, you men!" Captain Jennings barked.

Within minutes, the men were dressed and ready to leave the hospital, escorted by several officers armed with guns. The men were asked to place their hands on their heads whilst they were prodded in their backs with the guns like cattle off to market. It was obvious these men weren't being persuaded to go back to the Front, or asked to do so, they were prisoners of the army. The same army they had willingly signed up for, to defend their country. What a way to treat them. It incensed Adele so much, but what could she do?

"Is there really any need for this?" Adele pleaded with the captain. But her pleas fell on deaf ears, and both she and Morag, watched helplessly along with the other nurses and male orderlies, who were now awake, who did nothing to intervene. Adele guessed they feared being made to fight themselves if they did so, or else face a firing squad for obstructing a senior military officer.

When the soldiers and their charges had departed, all the staff settled the patients back down into their beds, who were baffled by all the commotion. Then Adele and all her staff sat in the large kitchen and drank copious amounts of tea until first light. There wasn't a dry eye between them, and they had little choice other than to carry on and attend to the remainder of the patients in their care.

Chapter Eight

The following day at the hospital, it was as if a cloud of despair was hanging all over their heads. The staff and patients were quite morose to think that several of their own had been returned, by force, to the trenches. Mr. Bellingham and Doctor Bowden showed up once they'd been told the news. Adele had got word to them via Arthur the stretcher bearer, when he'd transferred a patient from the clearing station earlier. She trusted Arthur, who was disgusted when he'd heard what had happened.

"I don't understand it meself," he said, removing his helmet and scratching his bald head. "Anyone could see that Donald and the others ain't right." He shook his head sadly and took the letters Adele had written to Mr. Bellingham and Doctor Bowden, from her outstretched hand.

An emergency meeting was held later that afternoon, where they discussed what could be done about future cases of shell shock at the hospital.

"I think," said Mr. Bellingham, "we need to get these cases back to Britain as soon as possible. It's a shame that we can't treat them here first for as long as I'd like, but I recommend that the team including Doctor Bowden, Adele and you Morag, as part of the nursing team, return back home with as many men as soon as possible who are suffering from shell shock, and continue the talking cure and other therapies there. Then I'll try to get shipments of men sent from here on a regular basis. I know of someone who's doing marvellous ground breaking work with the men in hospitals at Hampshire and Devon."

Everyone at the hospital was in agreement. It was a pity that it was too late for the likes of Donald and the other men.

***

And so a few weeks later, Adele, Doctor Bowden and Morag, found themselves at The Netley Hospital in Southampton, Hampshire. The Royal Victoria Military Hospital at Netley was not only England's biggest building, and a grand one at that, but also its 'largest palace of pain'. A large Red Cross hutted hospital was built at the back of the main hospital to accommodate around 2,500 beds. Most of the staff were Red Cross volunteers. Major Arthur Hurst, who had volunteered for service with the Royal Army Medical Corps, after establishing a neurology department at Guy's Hospital in London, was instrumental at this hospital. He'd been to France to see the work doctors there were doing with men diagnosed as suffering from 'hysteria' and was able to travel on to witness the horrors at Gallipoli, before returning to England to put new treatments he had learned into practice. Hurst helped men at the Netley and Seale Hayne hospitals get well again, by introducing hypnosis, talking cures, occupational therapy and writing too, by even producing their own hospital magazine, with a gossip column called, 'Ward Whispers'. He also filmed the men so improvements could be viewed at a later date.

Adele found Major Hurst's treatment and findings very interesting. His miracle treatments meant that he was able to cure 90% of shell-shocked soldiers in just one session. She had never seen anything like it in her life and was allowed to view the treatments at Seale Hayne Hospital which included: taking the men out into the countryside and helping out on a farm. He got them to relive the battlefield of Flanders on Dartmoor, and encouraged them to try firing a rifle again. His methods were ground breaking, before this, military treatments had been harsh and included solitary confinement, electro convulsive therapy and disciplinary treatment, whereas Major Hurst concentrated on the men's well-being by introducing dietary changes and massage, employing a more holistic approach to healing, which seemed to work very well.

Adele wrote to James Bellingham to tell him all about the Major's treatment of the shell-shocked soldiers and how he treated them with dignity and humanity. She was so excited about it all, but she missed working with James so much and that afternoon they'd spent picnicking in Northern France, was never far from her mind.

Meanwhile, Morag was pining for Donald, she'd not heard anything from him even though Arthur the stretcher bearer had passed on the hospital address to him. So Adele asked James in her letter if he'd heard anything from Donald, or indeed any of the other four soldiers who had been suffering from shell shock.

It was while she was at the hospital that her parents came to visit her. She was given the day off and she fell into her mother's arms. After all that time of keeping a stiff upper lip in Belgium and France, now she felt like a young child again. Her parents clinging to her and sobbing to see their daughter was safe and well for themselves.

"Oh, it's so good to see you again, Adele," Her mother hugged her tightly. Then between sobs, "I...thought you'd...never return from France. We were so worried about you."

She gazed into her mother's watery eyes, she looked a little older and weary worn. Had she put her parents through too much by going overseas to a war zone?

Her father patted her shoulder, "Come on young lady, after all you've been through, out there and over here, you deserve a medal, but would a pot of tea and some fancies do? Your mother spotted a lovely looking tea room on the way here."

Adele nodded gratefully, it was such a relief to be grounded with her parents once more. She watched as her father wiped away a tear. That steely, determined man, who hardly showed his emotions was crying a tear of happiness.

The afternoon went well after a tea of thinly sliced cheese and cucumber sandwiches and a selection of miniature cakes, they went for a stroll in a nearby park, and all too soon, time began slipping away, but not before she'd had chance to ask about the family.

"And how are Grandma and Grampa?" she enquired.

"Grandma is fine," her mother said, "but..." Her mother's voice held a catch to it.

"But what?" Adele's lower lip trembled.

"It's your Grampa, Adele...we kept it from you, but he died a couple of months ago."

Adele suddenly felt as if all the breath had gone out of her body, not her dear Grampa, no, it couldn't possibly be true. She swallowed hard, took in a deep breath and let it out again, to compose herself. "But why didn't anyone write to tell me?"

Her father stood in front of her and placed his hands on her shoulders, and whilst gazing into her eyes said, "Would it really have helped to know your grandfather had died when you were dealing with death on a daily basis on the Front Line, my dear?" He relaxed his stance and softly caressed her cheek. All of a sudden, she felt like a little girl, not a grown-up, trainee doctor, who had helped save so many lives.

She knew, of course, her father was right. He hugged her closely to him and allowed her to weep into his shoulder.

"Your grandfather is buried in Cefn Cemetery," her mother said soothingly. "Next time you're back home, we'll take you to visit his grave, you can pick some flowers from the garden to place there. And we'll take you to see Grandma Kathleen too..." She softly stroked her daughter's head.

Adele nodded. "I'd like that." She noticed how her parents had waited until the end of their visit to inform her that Grampa had died and thought it most thoughtful of them to do so.

"What happened?" she managed to ask when she'd finished crying, and drew away from her father's embrace.

Her mother draped an arm around Adele. "Your grandmother went out shopping one day, Grampa seemed fine when she left him, but when she returned, she thought he was asleep in the armchair but he'd passed away. Seemed as though he'd died in his sleep."

Adele sniffed. "I suppose that's the best way to go after what I witnessed overseas, just peacefully during your sleep, blissfully unaware of anything or the fact you're leaving anyone behind." She stiffened a moment. "What about his twin brother, Delwyn, has he been informed?"

"We immediately sent word to him and Rose, via a telegram, and they returned one to us to confirm that they'd received it, sending their condolences." Her father explained. "Of course, it was too far a journey for them to come all the way from Utah, and at their ages, too. Your mother and I sent another wreath on behalf of him and Rose. They were very close as young lads, your grandmother said. Inseparable, and although they were identical twins, they were as alike in their ways as chalk and cheese!"

Adele smiled through a haze of tears. "Yes, Grandma did tell me that! At least Grampa got to spend some time in Utah with his brother, even if it was many years ago, and they always wrote to one another, I hear."

Her mother nodded. "Yes, yet circumstance dictated they lived miles away from one another. Your grandfather loved your grandmother so much he returned from Utah to find her again."

Adele nodded. There were sad tears for all of them, but she knew her grandfather had led a useful life, both as a coal miner and later as a policeman with the Glamorgan Constabulary.

"I shall write to Grandma tonight," Adele said firmly. "And I'll tell her I'll be visiting her soon."

"That's the spirit," her father said. "Now before we go back to Wales, we're going to take you out for a nice meal a little later, you're getting far too thin for my liking my girl, no meat on those bones!"

She giggled. It was so good to be with both her parents once more, but she was sorry too that she had no more leave from work. Soon she would be expected to return to her training at the Royal Free London Hospital.

Before Adele was to return however, she was allowed leave back to her home town of Merthyr Tydfil, travelling by train, where she immediately went to see her grandmother.

The once neat little garden was now overgrown with weeds. Adele's grandfather had taken pride in the garden but now she guessed that her grandmother had neither the inclination nor the aptitude to see to it herself. The once freshly painted doors and windows of the house were scuffed and the paint peeling off. She made a mental note to ask her father to attend to it, now there was no man around the house any longer.

Adele stood on the doorstep, hesitating before knocking on the door, then she rapped with the knocker three times. It was some time before the door drew open and there, stood her lovely grandmother, Kathleen, all dressed in black in a high ruffled dress. Her face lit up as soon as she saw it was her granddaughter who stood there. Her emerald eyes shining from her pale worn face.

"Come on in, child," she beckoned warmly. "I knew you were going to visit after I received your letter but I didn't think t'would be today!" She had lost none of her Irish accent.

Adele followed her grandmother into the house and out into the kitchen where she always liked to sit. She was still living in The Walk area of the town.

"Now sit down and tell me all about what happened out in France!" She exclaimed with a twinkle in her eye. "Did you get to meet any nice handsome French men?"

Adele shook her head and smiled as she took a seat opposite her grandmother.

"No, I didn't really get to meet any French men, Grandma, but I met a lot of soldiers, poor things."

"Aye, and I bet you saw some sad sights, too," her Grandma said.

Adele nodded. She didn't feel like discussing some of the things she'd seen, with anyone. It was hard to see men with torn limbs, some with parts of their skulls blown away or stomachs bayonetted, with intestines hanging out, it wasn't a job for the faint-hearted, that was for

75

sure. Yet, for all those physical wounds she'd encountered, it was the men who were shell-shocked that she found the hardest to deal with. Not because she couldn't, she could. It was just so emotional and heartbreaking.

When they'd chatted for a few minutes, Adele asked, "And how are you coping, Grandma?"

Kathleen shook her head. "I'm all right, 't'will all be all right, you'll see." She wiped away a tear with the back of her hand. "Your mother and father visit me regularly and the boys of course."

The 'boys' her grandmother mentioned were James her eldest son and twins, Benjamin and Daniel, who of course were no longer boys, but middle-aged men. "It's good to know everyone's keeping an eye on you!"

"Then, of course, there's my good neighbour next door, Bill. He's always been so kind to me."

Adele remembered Bill well, her own mother told her that Bill had grown close to her grandmother when her grandfather had left for pastures anew. He'd wanted to marry her but Kathleen's faith wouldn't allow it. She hesitated a moment as she felt like saying, "Well, there's nothing to stop you two marrying now..." But it was too soon, her grandmother was still grieving for her husband. Their relationship had been very turbulent over the years, that much was for sure.

"Come on Grandma, I'll make us a nice cup of tea," Adele said brightly. Her Gran was looking far too thin for her liking and she feared she wasn't looking after herself properly.

She made her grandmother a mutton stew and a rice pudding before she left. They would last her a couple of days and would be easy for her to digest. Maybe it was time they paid someone to take care of her now she was all alone.

***

The following day, Adele stood with her mother at the grave of Dafydd Jenkin at the Cefn Coed Cemetery. It was a windy day, though the sky was quite blue, save for a few white fluffy clouds. He'd been laid to rest under a large tree near the entrance. So far, no gravestone had been laid as the earth needed time to settle. So there was just a small wooden cross with his name on and date of birth and death.

Adele knelt and laid a bouquet of lilacs and lilies on his grave. "Farewell, Grampa," she whispered, "till we meet again..."

She stood and her mother touched her shoulder gently, as if to say all would be well. The clouds parted and the sun shone through the leaves in the tree. It was a lovely spot to be laid to rest, Adele thought, feeling much better she'd been to the grave.

"When you're home next, there will be a proper headstone in place," her mother said.

That comforted Adele greatly. She stayed another few days in Merthyr before returning to Devon.

***

When she got back to the hospital, she found Morag running towards her. "We've got mail!" she said excitedly. "Both of us, from France!"

Adele knew what was going through Morag's mind, a letter from Donald. Adele realised her letter would be from James Bellingham.

Morag handed her letter to Adele, "Go on, read it now, I don't know if I can read mine, you might have to do it for me!"

Adele smiled nervously hoping it wouldn't be bad news for either of them. She opened the buff envelope and unfolded the letter that was written using beautiful penmanship.

"My Dearest Adele,

I hope things are going well for you at the Devon hospital. Things haven't been so good at this end." Her stomach lurched with fear and dread. *"The men took some severe artillery fire last night and 32 of them were killed, including some of the stretcher bearers. I'm afraid, Arthur, our favourite one of all, didn't make it. I'm told he died instantly which is a blessing..."* Adele's voice trailed away as she watched Morag's bottom lip quiver. *"I'm sorry to tell you, I have no idea what happened to the five men you mentioned. I have not come into contact with any of them since they left the hospital. Doctor Bowden is still working with the shell-shocked men and we are planning to despatch some more of them to England soon. Oh, when will this awful war end because then my darling..."*

"Sorry, I better not read any more, it's personal," she informed Morag. "I'm so sorry to hear what happened to poor, old Arthur though, he was a gem."

Morag shook her head. "The best way to look at it is, look how many lives he probably managed to save by getting the soldiers to us at the clearing station and hospital."

Adele had to admit, her friend was right. At the end of the day,

77

Arthur's presence on the Front Line, transferring the wounded soldiers, had affected a lot of people.

Morag smiled through her unshed tears as she handed Adele her letter.

"Are you sure you want me to read this one, it might be bad news?" Adele asked.

Morag nodded. "I know, but I need to know if he's dead or alive!"

Adele slipped her own letter into her jacket pocket and opened Morag's and read.

"My dear sweet Nurse Morag..."

Her eyes went to the end of the letter to ensure it was from Donald and it was. "Donald's alive! At least he was alive when he wrote this!" she exclaimed excitedly.

Morag ripped the letter from Adele's hands and excitedly read:

"I'm coping quite well at the moment, the hope of seeing you again, spurs me on. The thought that one day we will see one another again after this blessed war. I long to hold you in my arms and kiss your red lips."

Morag blushed and read the rest of the letter silently to herself. Tears now streaming down her face, she hugged Adele as both women shared a beautiful moment, realising that the men they thought so much of were still alive.

That night, Adele penned a letter to James telling him all about her parents' visit and how her grandfather had died without her knowing about it. She also informed him that to her knowledge Donald was still alive as Morag had received word from him. Though she was so sorry to hear what happened to Arthur. *"Soon I shall return to my training in London and I hope to see you when this blessed war is over..."* She refrained from signing it with all her love, as she held that feeling in check, after all, they might never see one another again.

Morag stayed on working at the hospital with the other Red Cross nurses, whilst Adele returned to her digs at London. As she stood staring at the house, she wondered how she'd adapt to going back to the Royal Free Hospital. The silly complaints and niggles from her male contemporaries paled into insignificance now, after all that had happened out in France and Belgium.

Belinda was there to greet her when she arrived, excited and full of life trying to tell her two things at the same time, whilst Mrs Gibson stood there smiling. "Come in Adele, we were expecting you!" she enthused. "Your benefactor paid to keep your room open for you all this time!"

Naively, Adele assumed that Mrs Gibson would have kept it open for her anyway as she was serving the war effort, but Edna was a widow and it would have affected her deeply to lose payment for the room month-upon-month.

"Benefactor?" she blinked several times.

"Yes, Oliver Worthington called here the night you left to explain he wanted your position here kept open, he has been keeping up the payments on a monthly basis, my dear. Didn't you know?"

Adele's face flushed as she shook her head. *Oliver!* She'd hardly paid him a thought since receiving that letter from James where he laid his heart on his sleeve for her. "T...that's so kind of him..." she wanted the ground to swallow her whole at that point. To be beholden to someone else, in a way made her angry, and gave her a sense of humiliation.

As if realising this, Edna spoke softly. "Doctor Worthington was only being kind to you, Adele...you could hardly expect me to keep your room going for you without any payment."

"I'm sorry, Mrs Gibson," she shook her head almost near to tears. "My mind was so intent on serving overseas, it was the last thing on it. Of course, it was a kind gesture for Doctor Worthington to pay to keep it open for me as else you'd have lost rent on it if unoccupied. I shall thank Oliver myself when I see him, but I intend to repay him every last penny!" She straightened her countenance, she was a proud woman who liked to stand on her own two feet.

"Now come along!" Belinda chirped. "Let's all have a nice cup of tea and you can tell us all that went on in France, the things you never told me in any of your letters!"

Adele smiled. It was good to be back home.

***

Back at the hospital with Belinda the next day, she found herself in a powerful position, the other male students now held her in high regard asking her questions like, "Did you really get to perform all those amputations?" and another popular question was, "How did you cope with all that death?" She got pats on the back from the young men and admiring glances from the women, who claimed they couldn't have done the same thing at all.

After a lecture on the digestive system given by Doctor Woodrow-

Smythe who was pleased to see her back home and spent the first few minutes extolling her virtues, she remained behind to find out what she needed to catch up on with regards to her studies, as she had been away for months.

"I wouldn't worry too much about it, Adele," he said in a kindly fashion, "you've learned more in those few months than that lot just gone from here have in a whole year! I've put together some notes for you just to brush up on, that should be enough. Oh, and you missed just one examination, I've put you down to sit that one next month."

She nodded politely. "Thank you."

"Oh, before you go," he said, calling her back, "Doctor Worthington would like to see you in his office."

Apprehensively, she walked towards the room, her heart beating wildly and with some trepidation, she tapped softly on his office door.

"Enter!" he called out.

His eyes lit up when he saw her standing there.

"My dear, Adele," he drew close to her and took both her hands in his own, gently kissing both cheeks. "I've missed you so much."

Her cheeks flamed, not quite knowing how she felt. She did have feelings for the man, but he was so much older than herself and now, James Bellingham had revealed his intentions, she was so confused.

"I've missed you too, Oliver. Has much happened since I've been away?"

He smiled and gestured her to take a seat. "Not as much as what's happened where you were stationed, it must have been horrendous?"

She nodded, then sat opposite him while he sat behind his desk. "It was, but somehow I got through it all."

He raised a silvery brow. "You do yourself a disservice, my dear. It took someone with great mettle to work very near to a war zone. It's not for the faint-hearted."

She smiled. People were making her out to be some sort of heroine, but she didn't see herself that way at all. "I just did my job, that's all, anyone else would have done the same thing." She answered modestly.

Mr. Worthington's eyes lit up as if to say, 'I so admire you, Adele' and she lowered her gaze. "Now tell me," he said, "how are you finding it being back here?"

"Not too bad, but it's taking some getting used to as I've been working mainly with shell-shocked patients at the Netley and Seale Hayne hospitals..."

"I see. And what happened?" He sat forward with interest in his seat.

"Well when I left France and arrived in Hampshire, I was told there was a doctor at the hospital who specialised in the treatments of shell-shocked soldiers, so I spent a lot of time studying his work and shadowing him. The medical profession could learn so much from his approach."

"In what sort of respect do you mean?"

"Well instead of treating the men as malingerers, as though they are putting things on, he believes in a talking cure and getting them to relive their torment. He's even got some to fire a rifle again. Of course, the treatment and them getting well is a double-edged sword as often if they are deemed fit enough, they get sent straight back out to the Front Line. He maintains that the men are suffering from a huge trauma. I've seen some amazing things. Men who had gone blind or deaf, seeing and hearing again. It's because some are so wracked with guilt their minds turn against their bodies."

Oliver Worthington paused, "It does sound most interesting I admit, though there are many at this hospital who would pooh pooh such treatment."

"Mr. Bellingham was very open to the talking cure out in France. He witnessed its success first hand. In fact, I think it should be employed here if we get any cases of shell shock."

"We've had a few we haven't known what to do with. I got really annoyed one day as some of those 'white feather women' walked on to one of the wards and started handing out feathers to the poor men!"

Adele's jaw dropped. "What happened?"

"Matron soon gave them a tongue lashing I can tell you! Those women ought to be horsewhipped!"

"I couldn't agree with you more. Haven't those men suffered enough?"

"We need to ensure the men aren't traumatised any further by that sort of thing." Oliver's eyes widened. "By Jove, I think I have an idea. Maybe we could convert one of the wards especially for that very purpose and employ the 'talking cure' and other therapies that you've spoken of. I would lead the team, so we'd get to work closely together. I'd have to put it to the hospital board, of course..."

She could see his mind ticking over and was excited about the idea herself but, there was just one small problem, James Bellingham wanted her to wait for him. That's what he'd proposed in his letter that she hadn't shown Morag. What if by working with Oliver, he got the wrong idea? She already felt beholden to him for rescuing her from Hubert Tavistock's clutches that time, not to mention paying several months' rent to keep her room open for her at Mrs Gibson's boarding house.

He gazed intently at her for a moment, then lifting her chin with his forefinger, so she was forced to look into his eyes, asked, "But what is the matter, Adele? Don't you like my idea?"

Much to her surprise, her eyes began to fill with tears and she swallowed hard. "It's not that..."

"Then just what is it?" he asked gently.

"It's James Bellingham, we drew close to one another when we worked together in France. He's written to me to ask me to wait for him."

There was a long silence as Adele thought she saw Oliver swallow down his disappointment, but then in quite a professional manner he said, "Not to worry about that, we shall keep our relationship on a professional basis only. I'm too old for you anyhow..." He turned away to gaze out of the window.

She stood behind him. "It's not that," she said softly. "I hadn't thought of becoming involved with any man at this present time, but war changes people. It's made me realise that we can be here one moment and gone the next. I've decided that when my training is over, I would like to settle down and have children, and then maybe return to the profession, or return part time. I got the impression from you that you've lived alone for so long it would be quite alien to you to have a house full of children."

He turned toward her and closing the space between them, gently took her in his arms, so that she was looking up at him. "Oh Adele, you are so very wrong. From the first moment I saw you, I knew that I loved you..." He hesitated for some time before bringing his lips crashing down on hers, at first she wanted to fight him off but felt powerless to resist and so succumbed to his fervent kisses, as her bosom swelled with the love she'd had a long time for him and hadn't realised until now.

"Please tell me," he said, when he finally broke away, "that you feel the same way, too?"

She nodded, her head was swimming with desire for him. "Yes, I do. I believe I love you too, Oliver."

"Then let's not wait a moment longer, let's get married. Please Adele, take me home to Wales with you when you next visit and I can ask your father for your hand in marriage."

Breathlessly, she whispered. "Yes, Oliver, I'd like that..."

Chapter Nine

A fortnight later, Adele and Oliver took the train from London to Cardiff and then another from Cardiff to Merthyr Tydfil. Adele had already written to her parents to say they would be arriving, but she had no idea what sort of a reception they'd receive. So it was with some trepidation she entered her old family home, as the maid let them in.

Oliver looked all around him. "This really is a lovely house, Adele," he enthused.

She smiled. "Yes, it's a lovely house, but this would fit into a corner of your home, Oliver."

He twiddled his moustache and with a twinkle in his eye said, "Very soon my home shall be your home and it shall be filled with love and laughter."

At that point her mother and father appeared from the drawing room, looking extremely pleased to see them. They were both ushered into the drawing room where the women took a glass of sherry and the men drank port, with her father pumping Oliver's hand as a way of introduction. Adele was relieved to see both men getting on so well. Oliver wasn't as old as Doctor Owen, but at his age, he could be mistaken for her father.

She smiled as she heard them speak about all things surgical and also from time-to-time, discussing the Great War.

Her mother whispered in her ear. "So, why have you really brought Oliver Worthington to visit us?"

"He wishes to speak to Father later."

"Is he about to ask for your hand in marriage?" she asked in jest.

Adele paused, then let out a long breath before answering, "Actually, yes."

Her mother's jaw dropped. "I was only joking with you. Oh Adele, he is so much older than you."

"I know, but then again there's a large age gap between you and father."

"I was just thinking that life could become hard for you in later years when you might have to take care of him."

Adele patted her mother's hand. "Please do not fret. We are in love with one another and that's all that matters."

Her mother smiled. "It seems as though you have made up your minds. Just give me the word and you and I shall go for a walk in the garden to leave the men alone to talk."

Adele agreed, and then it was another hour before she nodded to her mother for them both to depart the room, leaving Oliver alone with her father.

Half an hour later, both men emerged with big smiles on their faces. Her father had a cigar in his hand, he only smoked a cigar on a special occasion. "Come on, Mother!" He bellowed. "Mr. Worthington has asked for our daughter's hand in marriage and I've agreed!"

Of course, Adele had spoken a lot about Oliver Worthington and with great affection too, since being at the hospital—so her parents thought of him as being a kind and caring gentleman.

Her mother nodded and smiled, not giving away the fact she already knew what was going on.

"Oh splendid!" her mother said, bringing both palms of her hands together. She stood in front of Oliver and looking directly into his eyes said, "I hope you'll bring my daughter much happiness and she you!"

Oliver smiled almost in a nervous fashion.

Was that Adele's imagination or did her mother almost threaten Oliver? It was almost as though she was saying to him, "You be on your best behaviour Oliver Worthington, or you'll have me to contend with!"

Dismissing her feeling as foolishness, Adele stood by her father's side and said, "I'm so glad you agreed, Father."

Her father, who would do anything for her, beamed. "Now come along all of you, we must celebrate this very grand occasion. I'm going to take you all out to a nice restaurant I know for a meal. Her father was going to spare no expense by the look of it and later that evening, they ended up sitting in a very classy establishment a few miles out of Merthyr, where the wine flowed and money was no object. Adele's mother had dropped her guard and now seemed to be warming to Oliver. She hoped they wouldn't be displeased that she and Oliver planned to marry as soon as possible. This blessed war seemed to put people in the moment as for some, there was no tomorrow. Adele realised herself, she could well have got injured or died overseas.

***

A couple of weeks later when preparations for the wedding were underway, Adele received a letter from James. It had taken a while to get through to her as it had been sent to the Sealy Hospital and Morag had forwarded it on to her to Mrs Gibson's residence.

Trembling, she slit open the envelope to read:

My Dearest Adele,

It is some time since I last heard from you. It has been hard going here, the men are becoming despondent as they feel this war will never end. I'm so glad you are back home, this is really no place for a woman. Only yesterday I treated someone who was in a terrible state both physically and mentally. He told me how he'd had to clamber over his dead comrades in order to run to safety, he didn't look down, until the end when his boot came down on the face of his best friend and pushed him further into the mud. He didn't even have the time to go back and pull his dead friend out. Those are the conditions these men are operating in, as you well know and I expect you are still seeing the aftermath for yourself.

Anyhow, it was hours before the stretcher bearers could even get to those men and then the young soldier I mentioned got to see his best friend and hold him in his arms. They had grown up with one another and known each other all of their lives. It broke my heart to hear their story, which I will tell you about when I return home.

You, my darling, are the only thing that keeps me going. My only hope for the future. Everything seems so futile here.

Please write back to me soon as your letters keep me going.

Yours forever,

James.

Adele felt a lump in her throat and a tear coursed her cheek. At that point she heard the front door open and slam shut. Belinda! She was always doing that, heavy-footed she flounced into Mrs Gibson's drawing room.

"Adele, I had a great meeting with the Suffragettes, I even stood up to speak and we..." she broke off mid-sentence and rushed over to Adele's side. "What's the matter? Have you had some bad news?" she asked, noticing the letter in Adele's trembling hand.

"Oh Belinda, what am I to do? I've promised to marry Oliver but James thinks I'm waiting for him."

Belinda's eyes widened. "Well, one thing's for certain...you can't go breaking everything off right now by letter, that man's mind might be affected by all he's seen and done. I'd reply to him, keep the letters going, there will be time enough when he returns home to end it with him. After all, it never really got started in the first place from what you told me?"

"You're right, nothing more than a shared kiss one time and I put a boundary in telling him it wasn't the time nor the place..."

"And that kiss was probably because war does funny things to people..." Belinda said wistfully.

Adele nodded. "You're right of course, but I feel bad duping him. If Oliver should ever find out, they were both colleagues at the hospital of course and will work together again sometime in the future. It's all such a complicated mess."

Belinda patted Adele's arm. "I know and understand. But you have to keep this going so James will have hope to get back home. I've heard of men taking their own lives out there due to all the sights they've seen, and it will be worst for James as he's on the Front Line between life and death, operating on them as well you know."

"I know you are right..." Adele sniffed. "I don't know why I agreed to wait for him in the first place, it wasn't until I saw Oliver again and realised how much he really cared for me, that I knew I loved him."

Belinda stood and said in a brusque, business-like manner, "Now, I want you to stop crying, Adele, it will do you absolutely no good. Wash your face and I'm taking you out to that Italian Ice cream parlour down the road. Then I'm going to bore you half to death telling you about what the Suffragettes are going to get up to next!"

Adele laughed, her friend never failed to cheer her up, in some ways she reminded her of Morag, but she was more forceful and independent. That reminded her, when they returned from the ice cream parlour, she was going to write letters both to James and Morag.

"Just give me a few minutes to tidy myself up and I'll come with you," she said cheerfully. "And no, you shan't bore me half to death with your Suffragette talk, I find it all rather interesting."

Later, as they sat eating vanilla ice cream in long glasses topped with fruit, Belinda said. "I have a rather good idea...what about if I reply to James's letters if you feel so bad about it?"

Adele set down her spoon, then blinked several times. "Oh, I don't know if I could allow you to do that on my behalf...in any case, how would your writing look the same as mine?"

"Oh, I'm a master at forgery, dear! When I was in boarding school I used to forge Mama's signature quite regularly to get out of activities I detested. 'Mama' would write to the headmistress saying I couldn't go horse riding as I had a weak spine or I couldn't attend ballet lessons as I had dropped arches!" She guffawed loudly, then her face took on a serious expression. "In a couple of weeks' time you are due to marry, you wouldn't want Oliver to find your letters written to James, would you? And even if you explained why you were doing what you were doing, would he really understand?"

She had to admit that her friend had a point. It was a real dilemma. "Very well then, Belinda, I'll pass the letter on to you and give you a sample of my handwriting to copy. If you could use Mrs Gibson's address as a return one." Adele bit her lip. "I really don't like doing this you know."

Belinda patted her friend's hand. "But ask yourself, what other choice do you really have, Adele? Are you willing to break a man's heart overseas? It's far better to break it when he returns home when he'll have his loving family and friends for support."

Adele nodded sadly, what other choice did she have? She toyed with explaining the situation to Oliver but would he truly understand? "The other option, of course, is not to reply," she suggested.

"No, I wouldn't do that!" Belinda said sharply. "Why allow the man to worry about you? He's got enough worry as it is!"

"Suppose you're right..." She replied reluctantly.

"You know I am. Now, let me tell you what happened at that meeting!" Belinda's eyes were glowing like two shiny lumps of coal, and even though she wasn't in the mood to listen, Adele did and quite soon, they both ended up giggling like two school girls at the exploits of the Suffragettes.

"It's not all fun like that, though..." Belinda explained. "A few of the women got arrested last week and carted off to Holloway Prison."

"Oh, do take care, Belinda!" Adele warned her friend. "I should hate to see something like that happen to you."

"Please don't worry. I feel so strongly about this cause I would happily go to prison for it!"

"Well, be careful anyhow, you wouldn't want anything to jeopardise your medical career."

"No, of course not and my parents would be so upset, I realise that, but it's so unjust that women aren't treated with the same respect as men are. When the *Representation of the People Act* was passed in February, it was a vast improvement, but it still only means women over the age of thirty can vote, so you and I have no say, even though we're undertaking a life and death job. It's wrong—that age needs to be lowered!" she said in defiance, her chin jutting out. "And even then, those women over thirty have to have a certain amount of property in order to vote. It's preposterous if you ask me. It's been estimated out of all women over that age, only 40 percent are eligible to vote! So us Suffragettes intend to keep on campaigning, you're welcome to join us, Adele. I could put a word in for you!"

"I think I have enough on my plate at this moment, but I shall think about it."

"Please don't think too long, we need someone like you! What makes my blood boil is the same act has abolished property and various other restrictions for men and now *they* can all vote from the age of 21, but us ladies have to wait another 9 years! And even then we have to own property. What poppycock! Please think about it, Adele!"

Adele smiled. Becoming a Suffragette was the last thing on her mind right now.

***

The day of Adele's wedding to Oliver approached, and it was arranged that the ceremony take place at St. Tydfil's Parish Church in Merthyr Tydfil. It was a glorious day with hardly a cloud in the sky, Adele knew she was doing the right thing as she sat in the carriage with her father to transport them to the church, pretty pink satin bows had been tied onto the doors. Doctor Owen owned an automobile, but he thought it best for the wedding day that Adele was transported to the church in an open-topped horse and carriage, in style.

Nothing or no one was going to spoil today for Adele. Mrs Gibson and Belinda had travelled all the way from London, but there was no one from Oliver's side present because his parents had already passed away and he had no brothers or sisters. She guessed if James had not been in France that he might have come along.

A thought of James waiting for her momentarily threatened to burst her bubble, but she immediately quashed the thought. As she arrived at the entrance to the church on her father's arm, she couldn't have been happier, and to see Oliver turn and gaze at her in awe at the altar, was the icing on the cake.

When they were joined as man and wife, people rushed out of the church to throw rice and wish them well, in the crowd stood Belinda with a face of steel. What was wrong? When things had quietened down and the photographer had taken some snaps, Adele walked over to her friend.

"What's the matter, Belinda?" she asked. Mrs Gibson was happily chatting to a lady stood beside her.

Belinda pulled a letter from her pocket. "It's a letter from James..." she whispered.

Adele's eyes widened. "Please put that away...not here right now..."

"But you have to listen to me, right now..."

"Why?"

"Because James has returned to London and he's expecting to see you!"

Adele's jaw dropped open. "Oh, no, what am I going to do?"

"How long will you be staying in Wales for?"

"For another week, we're heading off in my father's car to Porthcawl for a few days. My father has kindly loaned it to Oliver."

"I really don't know what to suggest, but James has said he will be back working at the hospital soon and surely someone there will tell him about this marriage. Maybe you'd better send him a telegram before someone spills the beans to him, if they haven't already."

"Look, there's no time to discuss it right now. We'll speak later!" Adele said angrily, snatching the offending letter from Belinda's hand before someone should notice their altercation.

Somehow Adele managed to get through the rest of the day, smiling and chatting to the wedding guests at the side of her husband, but it wasn't easy, and she cursed Belinda for bringing her the news.

***

Oliver drove them to a little guest house on the seafront at Porthcawl the following day, they'd spent their honeymoon night at The Bentley's Hotel in Merthyr. It was everything she'd dreamt it would be, apart from one thing, Oliver had been tender but he was unable to perform his manly duty in the bedroom, he'd held her afterwards and cried huge wracking sobs putting it down to tiredness and the emotion of the day. She didn't know what to do—this wasn't what she was expecting at all. She knew as a doctor that some men suffered from impotence, but hoped it was because he'd felt a pressure to perform on their wedding night. He wasn't that young anymore at the age of fifty-two, she realised that, but would she now have to spend the rest of her married life feeling unfulfilled?

Her mind turned to James, if she had waited for him, things would have been different. She was so confused. He was much younger than Oliver and probably would have wanted to start a family. It was too late for any regrets, she'd made her bed and now had to lie in it. What she needed to do now was limit any damage that could occur as a result of that letter, which she had destroyed. The best course of action, she decided, was to confess to Oliver. He would be distressed about it, that much she knew for sure, but she had to tell him before they returned to London to face both James and the music. After all, she reassured herself it wasn't even as though she'd had a passionate affair with James, it was Belinda leading him on with those blessed letters. Silently, she cursed her friend for being so foolhardy and getting carried away with the romance of it all. They said their goodbyes to her parents for time being and set off to Porthcawl, Oliver blissfully unaware that anything was amiss.

So she chose the following morning, after a hearty breakfast at the guest house, to break the news to her husband. She'd hardly been able to finish her food, but Oliver had tucked into his bacon, fried egg and mushrooms with relish and even asked for another egg. After a rest and then a walk along the beach, she turned to him and said, "Oliver, there's something I need to say to you..."

He stopped a moment. A sea breeze blew, ruffling her hair, so she had to tuck it beneath her cloche hat to prevent it from blowing across her face.

"Oh? Is it about last night, I am so sorry Adele..." his voice trailed away, taken away with the breeze. They had tried to make love again at the guest house, but yet again it was a failure.

"No, it's not about last night at all, it's about quite another matter in fact..."

"Yes?"

She hesitated. "You know when I worked with James in France?"

"Yes, how could I possibly forget?" he smiled, his kindly blue eyes creasing at the edges. A child flying a kite ran past with his mother in tow.

"Well, before I left France, we got close to one another, nothing more than a kiss occurred but when I worked at Sealy Hospital with the shell-shocked men, he sent me a letter revealing his feelings for me, I was so confused. I agreed to wait for him."

Oliver frowned. "Oh Adele, all this time you've loved James and not me?"

"Oh no, no, it's not like that at all, Oliver. I realised I had very deep feelings for you as soon as I saw you again and agreed to marry you, but I couldn't go about breaking James's heart while he was overseas and sounding so downhearted."

"I understand, I think. So you didn't put him straight?"

"No..."

"Hopefully by now, if you then stopped writing to him, he'll have got the message."

"That's the point though, I didn't. Well to be truthful, I did but..."

He raised a silvery brow. "I don't understand?"

"Forgive me, but Belinda offered to write to him on my behalf and told me to break off the relationship when he arrived back in London."

Her husband stood there in disbelief. "I can't believe my ears, Adele, that you and that friend of yours would do this to someone."

"But don't you understand, Oliver, if I'd written to say it was all over and I didn't intend waiting for James's return, then it would affect his state of mind and who knows what might have happened."

"No, quite frankly I don't, and I think it very cruel of you to lead the man on. He's a very good friend of mine, you have now driven a wedge between us." He turned on his heel and strode away from her, back in the direction of the guest house.

She felt like running into the sea but as it was early morning the tide was out. What had she done? And now she'd gone and upset Oliver, too. Turning, she ran after him, holding her hat on her head as the breeze blew hard off the sea.

"Wait, Oliver, please wait!" she pleaded.

He stopped and slowly turned. "I really feel I don't know what to say to you, Adele. You don't seem to be the person I married."

"I am honestly," she huffed out a breath. "Really, Belinda and I weighed up the options about James and she continued writing the letters, not me. Once I was in your arms in your office that time you and I were reconciled, I never wrote another letter to James, you have my word on that."

He gave her a hard stare, then his eyes crinkled at the edges and she knew all would be well. "Oh, Adele, what am I going to do with you?" His eyes brimmed over. "I should never want to lose you, you mean so much to me, but you have to get this sorted out. We shall meet with James together and explain."

Her heart thumped loudly. "Oh...I don't know if that would be a good idea?"

"Yes, honesty is the best policy in my book. Come on, we shall face this together," he held out his hand to her and she took it, feeling safe and secure. As long as she was with Oliver, all would be well. She just knew it.

***

After staying a few more days in Porthcawl, they returned the car to Adele's father, and after spending some time in Merthyr before departing, they took the long train journey back to London. It was with some apprehension that a meeting with James was arranged.

He sat there in Oliver's office, blinking profusely. "This is some sort of joke, surely?" he demanded of the pair.

"No joke, James. I'm sorry, but Adele and I are married."

It took James a while to digest the words. France and Belgium had scarred him badly. He now looked thin and gaunt, his eyes having a haunted expression about them. "But I don't understand, Adele was supposed to wait for me, she said so in her letters." He turned to Adele.

For the first time, she spoke out. "No, James. I never said that, you did."

"I have the letters to prove it, your last letter said you couldn't wait to be my wife."

Realisation suddenly dawned, Belinda had gone too far in the letters. "That wasn't me who wrote those last few letters after Sealy, James. It was Belinda. We both thought it was wise for you to have something to look forward to, so you'd feel better about things. It was a bit like holding up a candle of hope at the window for you."

"Candle of hope?" he said angrily, standing so violently that his wooden chair clattered to the floor. "Is that what you call it? You women have duped me good and proper. I was expecting to return home and settle down with you, Adele. It's all I have longed for." Then turning towards Oliver he said, "And you were supposed to be my friend, Oliver. How could you have allowed this kind of thing to happen?"

Before Oliver had a chance to explain, Adele butted in. "Please don't blame Oliver, he had no knowledge of this until a few days ago. He suggested we both meet with you to discuss this."

A flicker of light shone from James's eyes for the first time, he nodded at Oliver. "I knew you wouldn't let me down, Oliver, we've been friends for a long time."

"I'm truly sorry, James. I had no knowledge of what Belinda wrote in the last lot of letters to you, it sounds as if she was being overly romantic."

"Overly romantic? Is that what you call it..." James paced the room.

"Please sit yourself back down, James," Oliver said kindly. "You've had a bad shock. The ladies were well-intentioned, they were concerned about your safety and welfare while you were in a war zone, that was all."

James seated himself and appeared to relax for a while, letting out a long breath. "I suppose in retrospect it was well-intentioned, though I should like to speak to Belinda, whoever she is, about those last lot of letters. She should be an author that lady, the power of that particular prose!"

Adele stifled a giggle and then James laughed too, and quite soon they were all smiling and laughing. Oliver stood. "Come on," he said to James, "You could do with a stiff drink at the club."

James nodded. "Yes, I suppose so."

Adele looked at him. "I'm so sorry, James, and it was wonderful to work with you. You're an amazing surgeon."

James smiled. "Yes, it was good to have you as part of the team, Adele. I'm sorry I got carried away, I should never have put you in that position. Apology accepted by the way."

She smiled. "No apology necessary on your part. I shall arrange a meeting with Belinda for you, please go easily on her. You'll probably recognise her anyhow from being around the hospital, she's one of the medical students here."

"I guessed as much," he said, a smile appearing on his face. "I would very much like to meet with her."

"She's very headstrong mind, while we were in France, she joined the Suffragette Movement."

James chuckled and for a moment, Adele wondered what he was thinking, it was almost as though one of those electric light bulbs had exploded in his mind. "My sister, Arabella, has recently joined forces with the Suffragettes, so we should have plenty to talk about!"

Adele felt a sudden pang of jealousy and she didn't know why she should feel that way, for a couple of seconds James gazed into her eyes as if they were quite alone in the room together.

The moment was broken when Oliver said, "I think you and I could do with that stiff drink, old boy." James turned toward Oliver and nodded. "Adele, I hope you don't mind? I shall order a cab for you to get back to the house. We shan't be too long."

"No, I don't mind at all." She smiled to herself, realising all would be well thanks to her husband's honourable behaviour.

When she arrived back at the house, the housekeeper, Mrs Charlton, was there, fussing around.

"What's the matter?" Adele asked, as the woman ran this way and that as if looking for something.

"It's those bleedin' Suffragettes, Mrs Worthington, Ma'am. They've been marching around the place, causing trouble."

"Oh, what do you think they were marching about this time?" She hadn't been in touch with Belinda since returning to London, so was totally unaware.

"Still about voting rights for women. It's not that I object, and I can well see their point of view, I half agree with it myself, but do they have to cause so much trouble? The police were out in force earlier and some of them had run and hidden away on this property, hiding behind bushes. One of the women said she was a friend of yours, Ma'am." Mrs Charlton sniffed, "if you ask me they'd be better off not causing so much strife for folk. Several of them were carted away in a Black Maria to Holloway, I suspect. Or else just locked up at the nick."

"Oh dear. I do hope nothing's happened to Belinda."

"If yer don't mind me saying so, Ma'am, that's a right 'un you've got yourself involved with there. She'd be better stopping home and making 'er 'usband's tea."

"Belinda is a good sort, Mrs Charlton, believe it or not she comes from a good family and is training to be a doctor with me!"

"Outrageous!" Mrs Charlton said, turning on her heel and walking off towards the kitchen. She was obviously upset by it all, especially that a member of the medical profession could act in such a manner.

Adele removed her hat and jacket and hung them on a wooden stand in the hallway, and then went to the bedroom she shared with her husband. It was a big room that needed a feminine touch. Mrs Charlton had done her best, bless her, arranging pretty pink roses from the garden in a cut glass crystal vase, but it needed redecorating for Adele's tastes. She gazed out the window to see Mrs Charlton and the parlour maid pegging out the washing, her husband's pristine white shirts flapping in the breeze. It was a very pretty garden, bordered with thick green bushes and a large oak tree, with a well-trimmed lawn and colourful flowerbeds, tended to by Arnold the elderly gardener. Apparently, he had worked at the house for years, originally tending to the garden as a young boy for Oliver's parents.

Adele sighed as she watched the women. Of course, she was used to having servants at home back in Wales, but after being out in France, she was used to being her own woman and taking care of herself. Now she felt almost obsolete in her own home. She would be returning to the medical profession the following week, though her husband had wanted her to put her career on hold. "My dear, you have already been through so much near the battle zone, why don't you take a break?" He'd suggested.

But she knew in her heart if she gave up the profession right now and had his children, she might never return to her life as a doctor. Although she did worry so about Oliver's ability to father a child, he still had problems in the bedroom and could only on rare occasions achieve an erection and even then, penetration seemed impossible. She worried it would drive a wedge between them, but she reassured herself that she loved him so much, so why should it?

The following day, Adele arranged a meeting between James and Belinda about 'the letter business' as she put it. They met in a small cafe near the hospital and from Belinda's account they got on very well. Indeed, she seemed overawed by the eminent surgeon, though Adele had no clue whatsoever what James thought of Belinda, but the meeting appeared to placate both James and her husband.

Back at the hospital, the days took their usual format of lectures, going on ward rounds, watching various medical procedures and operations. One day, Doctor Woodrow-Smythe informed Adele that there would be a very special procedure taking place and she having the most experience of this, would be required to assist Mr. Bellingham. The patient was someone she knew, Hubert Tavistock, who had been sent back to Britain after being wounded in France. He'd taken a hit which injured his right arm and had suffered horrendous burns to his face.

Adele recoiled in shock, her breathing became erratic, her pulse pounded at the thought of treating someone like him. The very man who had caused so much problem for her. She knew she had to be professional though and must treat him like any other patient, and so consequently agreed to assist. The other medical students as they already knew him were not allowed to observe this operation, on his father's orders.

The operation went well, Hubert had to have his arm amputated half way up his forearm beneath his elbow. "It's a good thing..." James said, as he looked at her above his white mask. "It means we can eventually fit him with a hook, so he can at least lift things with that hand. In a way it's fortunate."

"Fortunate?" she asked.

A nurse in long blue dress, white apron and cap, bandaged up the wound while Mr. Bellingham observed.

"Yes, Tavistock is left handed, I'm informed. So at least he will have full use of his left hand."

It was in that moment that Adele's heart went out to Hubert Tavistock. If he had not been so intent on pulling that sly trick at his house party that time, then he would not have had to leave the medical profession and end up in France. Although it was none of her doing, it was all his own silly behaviour, she did feel a certain responsibility towards the man. But then again, she reminded herself, it was that episode with the opium and the wild party at his parents' home that had been the deciding factor in him joining the army. His father had been very strict about that, she wondered if he felt a certain responsibility towards his son's injuries?

But then again, many young men had been conscripted into signing up to fight for their country and before that, many were pushed into signing up by family members, even their own wives after all the poster campaigns throughout the country.

One recruitment poster that had stuck vividly in Adele's mind was of two women gazing out of an open window at passing soldiers, as a young child stood nearby. The poster read: 'Women of Britain say – "Go!"' She guessed the women were supposed to represent the soldier's wife and mother, the young child being his son. So chances were that Hubert would have felt obliged to sign up anyhow, even if not conscripted to do so. The men who refused to fight, due to their faith or for other reasons, were classed as 'Conscientious Objectors' and often ended up in prison for their beliefs.

The following day, she went to visit Hubert on the ward. He was extremely groggy from the pain relief, but sitting up in bed. When he saw her, his face changed to a grimace. Oh dear, this wasn't going to be easy. As she approached though, he forced a smile, it was then she realised he'd grimaced due to the pain.

"Hello. How are you feeling today, Hubert?" she asked.

His mouth opened and closed several times, without any words coming out. Then he found his voice. "As well as can be expected I suppose..." he said sadly. "I hear you assisted Mr. Bellingham with yesterday's operation?"

"Yes, I did."

"Gosh, I couldn't imagine any of the other medical students doing that." He grimaced again.

"Are you in pain, Hubert?" she asked. It gave her no pleasure to see him in great discomfort, the stump of his right arm heavily bandaged, elevated on a pillow, surrounded by a metal frame to keep the weight of the bedclothes off his arm. His face red raw where he'd been burnt, appeared to be slathered in some sort of ointment.

"To tell you the truth, yes, Adele..."

She lifted his chart at the end of the bed and studied it for a moment. "I'll have a word with Mr. Bellingham about increasing the dose of Laudanum."

He managed a wan smile. "Thank...you..." he gasped breathlessly.

She was about to turn and leave, when he said, "Adele, I am sorry you know." He looked at her with such pleading in his eyes.

"I know," she said kindly. "Let's leave the past where it should remain."

He nodded and closed his eyes, then she went in search of Mr. Bellingham.

James was in the corridor laughing with Belinda about something or other. They appeared to be getting on well with one another.

"Could I have a word with you in a moment about Hubert Tavistock?" she asked.

He nodded and Belinda left to carry on with her duties. "What is it?"

"The pain relief doesn't seem to be touching him. Is there any chance of increasing the dosage?"

He nodded. "I was afraid of that, he is quite a tall chap and well-built too. I'll increase it a little, but not too much, as I don't want him getting addicted to the stuff, especially as he was prone to a little opium smoking beforehand."

"That's a good point, I hadn't considered that. I do feel so sorry for the man, though."

"Oh, and why is that after all he put you through, Adele?"

"Well, after being ousted from this hospital following his antics, he was forced to join up as a commissioned officer, imagine going straight into battle!"

"Er, ahem, it wasn't quite like that. He had to undertake four month's training first in an Officer Cadet Battalion. He was only a Wartime Temporary Officer."

"But what about his military competence?"

"The army doesn't seem to worry about that. He's well educated and his father holds some sort of title, so he was deemed as being 'a cut above' other soldiers."

"But we know that wasn't the case at all!"

"Yes, I know that and so do you, but the British Army seem to think they know best! In my mind, a lot of these commissioned officers are bloody buffoons and although they've been Oxford or Cambridge educated, they have not got a clue. Who knows how many poor men have been led to their deaths as a result!"

Adele shuddered. "That's a sobering thought."

"Yes, very." James paused. "How is Oliver? Is he coping well with married life?" His eyes twinkled with merriment.

Adele guessed he was referring to their love life, but she couldn't be sure. The truth was their love life was almost non-existent and she was finding that hard to live with. "He said he loves being married to me!" She replied in a haughty fashion.

"And who wouldn't..." James replied with a grin. "I missed my chance, that was for sure."

"You seem to be getting on well with Belinda?"

"Oh yes, we do get on so well with one another, I'm taking her to the theatre tonight."

Adele arched her eyebrows. "I didn't know Belinda liked the theatre."

"She's not that fussed usually, but there's a play on called, 'The Empowerment of the Working Class Woman'. She's been yearning to see it for a while, as it's the story of a young Suffragette. It's not really my cup of tea, but anything to keep a lady happy. Actually, I have sympathy for them due to Arabella's involvement. I'm glad you introduced me to Belinda, she's an amazing person!"

For a moment, Adele felt another flicker of jealousy and wished it was herself he was taking to see the play. Oliver never had the time to take her out these days, he spent hours at his gentleman's club, or at hospital meetings. Marriage wasn't quite what she was expecting it to be.

"Well, I hope you both have a good time," then as if to change the subject, Adele carried on, "I think it would be wise to see to Hubert's medication as soon as possible, James."

A few months ago before going to France, as a medical student, Adele would never have dreamed of addressing James by his Christian name, but as they'd worked so closely together, often with the big guns thundering in the distance, it seemed to have removed that barrier.

He searched her eyes for a moment. "Please tell me that you are happy, Adele?"

She swallowed for a moment. "Of course I am," she replied, her voice trembling.

"Then I'm happy for you, and although I feel that Hubert Tavistock should suffer a little for what he did to you and those other female students, I have an obligation as his surgeon to see to his pain relief. Thank you for letting me know. I respect your professional opinion."

Adele nodded and turned away from him hoping he couldn't see the blush that flamed her cheeks. She was glad to have returned to work at the hospital, but it was difficult seeing both men she cared so deeply for, almost every day.

As her footsteps echoed down the corridor she knew that James was standing there watching her departure. He still had feelings for her, that much was evident, and deep down she knew he doubted she was happy with her husband.

Chapter Ten

Belinda was most excited about the play she'd seen the previous evening, with James. "Yes, it was all about this Suffragette, she was a bit like me really, she didn't agree with 'The White Feather Movement' one tiny bit. She was torn as she'd fallen in love with this principled young gentleman, who turned out to be a Conscientious Objector. You can imagine the strife it caused. On one hand she wanted to protect him but on another, she thought she ought to persuade him to sign up and fight for his country..."

"That sounds interesting," Adele said. "What happened at the end of the play?"

"Oh, she persuaded him to sign up all right, and to do it for her and the women of the country, but he got shot in the Battle of Passchendaele."

Adele frowned. "That's very sad, Belinda."

"Yes, it is. But it wasn't a sad ending, in time he returned home to England. They married and lived the proverbial, 'Happy Ever After'. It got me thinking though about how people sometimes assume all Suffragettes agree with Emmeline Pankhurst, but she joined forces with that anti-feminist woman regarding the white feathers. Emmeline's daughters totally disagreed with her actions."

Adele placed her hands on both hips. "And so they should and all. It's awful what's been happening, young men signing up underage, and for what? To be used as cannon fodder. This is the most senseless war I've ever known!"

Belinda touched her friend's shoulder. "You know that more than most, Adele, after being out in Ypres and seeing casualties from the Battle of Passchendaele for yourself. After our shift today, shall we go to the ice cream parlour?"

Adele nodded. "I'd like that very much indeed." A sudden pang of envy took Adele as she thought of her friend being in the company of James Bellingham, whilst she was now married to a much older man who was becoming increasingly distant from her, both inside and outside of the bedroom.

A letter arrived from Morag who had such exciting news to tell, Donald was home from Ypres and they were getting married. She was extremely excitable about the whole thing and she invited Oliver and Adele to the wedding where she asked them both to be witnesses. It was to be a small low-key affair, as it would be too costly for her family to travel all the way from Dundee. Donald had no family to speak of, he was an only child and both his parents were dead.

Later that day, when she spoke about the invitation to Oliver, he seemed less than impressed.

"Do we really have to attend?" he asked, as he looked at her over the top of *The Times* newspaper as they sat at the table waiting for Cook to send in their evening meal.

"Well, I should very much like to attend, I was very close to Morag when we worked together under extreme duress, and I looked after Donald, too. We thought that time he was removed from the hospital and forced to go back to the Front, we'd never see him again!"

He let out a long sigh and folded his newspaper. "Oh, very well," he said, sitting back in his chair. The polished walnut table was a long one and they were seated opposite ends. It was far more formal here than back home.

"You spoke to me then as if placating a small child," she said sharply.

"It's not that, dear. It's just I have something else on at the same time, a meeting at my Gentleman's club. It is important, but I suppose I'll have to put it off now."

He was making her feel as though she were asking for the moon and that really annoyed her. "Don't trouble yourself," she said finally. "I could ask Belinda to go in your place."

"Very well, that's a good idea that would suit us both."

At that point, Nellie, one of the servants brought in the first course, which was leek and potato soup topped with a swirl of fresh cream. Although previously Adele had been ravenous. and the soup smelled delicious, she'd now lost her appetite for it. As she gazed around the dining room with its dark, wooden walls, adorned with works of art and the mounted head of a stag, she felt her eyes fill with unshed tears. This wasn't the life she imagined for herself, where her husband was more involved with his Gentleman's club than with her. Then she felt a sliver of guilt, telling herself that Oliver had lived alone for such a long time he wasn't used to doing things as a couple and his recent poor performances in the bedroom, might be making him depressed. She swallowed down a sob and forced herself to eat her soup. He failed to notice just how upset she really was.

By the time the main course of steak pie and vegetables arrived, she felt a little better and both were making small talk. Whilst they were finishing their desserts of apple pie and cream, Reeves, the butler, walked into the room.

"There's a gentleman by the door for you, Sir," he said, addressing Oliver.

"A gentleman?" Oliver wrinkled his nose. "But I don't have an appointment to see anyone this evening. What's his name?"

"Tedstone, Sir. Wally Tedstone."

At the mention of the man's name, Oliver's face reddened. He threw his cotton napkin onto the table and pushed his chair back forcefully to stand. "I'll sort this out Reeves, you help Nellie clear the table when my wife has finished her meal."

"Very well, Sir." Reeves gave her a look and a shrug that said, "I really don't know what's going on."

"I'm sorry, Adele," Oliver said, "you carry on without me." He left the room, marching purposely to meet with the man.

Adele stood herself to make her way to the bedroom and was surprised when she saw no sign of the gentleman nor her husband in the hallway talking as she expected, she thought maybe they were in the drawing room, so made her way upstairs. When she got to the landing, she gazed out the window down below to the garden, only to see her husband in some sort of heated discussion with a very handsome young man. He reminded her of one of those Renaissance painters with their long, curly hair, that was unusual for most men to sport these days. He wore a white high neck shirt with shiny green cravat and long Velvet black jacket. He was what her mother would have described as a 'dandy', beneath his arm he carried a cane.

Oliver was pointing a finger at him, appearing as if he was telling him to leave his property. Then much to her dismay, the younger man hunched over and began to weep in quite a dramatic fashion, as Oliver appeared to relent and pat his back. Then looking around in all directions, but not up at the window, Oliver dug into his pocket and appeared to give the man some money and showed him out through the back garden gate.

Adele drew a breath. What had just gone on there? She hadn't a clue. It appeared maybe the younger man was blackmailing her husband. But why? One thing was for sure, Oliver was shocked he had shown up at the house at all and that unnerved her greatly.

When Oliver returned back indoors, his face was pale and worry lines had appeared on his forehead.

"Is there anything the matter?" she asked, as she stepped off the bottom step of the ornate staircase.

He shook his head vigorously. "Just some young man asking for a donation for a charity."

She drew a breath of composure. It didn't look like that at all to her. That young man was very upset about something and she intended to find out what that something was. "I see," she replied, walking past her husband to the drawing room, where she sat in a high back armchair and gazed out the long French windows into the garden. Though she didn't see at all. Something was amiss, she was sure of it.

***

Adele told Belinda of her concerns the following day. "I'm sure that young man is blackmailing, Oliver. I saw my husband handing over money to him."

Belinda looked at her wide-eyed, they were both on a lunch break at the hospital and sitting in the grounds on a bench, eating some of Mrs Gibson's apple pie that she'd made for the pair of them, she still liked to keep an eye on Adele, and was the nearest person she had as a mother figure in the whole of London.

"Yes, but if as you say, Oliver mentioned it was something to do with charity, then maybe he handed the money over to get shot of the young man."

Adele bit her lip. "No, it was far more than that, Belinda. The man looked upset with my husband for some reason, close to tears."

"But how could you tell all that as you told me you were watching from the bedroom window?"

"I was. I saw the man fall to his knees and put his head in his hands as if succumbing to complete devastation."

Belinda frowned. "That sounds very strange indeed, Adele. I think you need to ask your husband what's going on. Shall I ask James to have a word with him?"

Adele shook her head vehemently. "Oh, no, please. It's something I have to sort out for myself. Maybe they had a chat about it last night at the club anyhow."

Belinda blinked several times. "I hardly think so—James was with me all evening. We went for a stroll to the park, then back to Mrs Gibson's for a cup of tea. You know how she likes making a fuss over people." Belinda chuckled.

Though Belinda thought last night was quite humorous, Adele did not. Oliver had told her he'd gone to the club and that he'd been in James's company all night long. Quashing the thought, she tried to concentrate on something else. Something more worthwhile. She was just about to ask Belinda if she'd like to come over for dinner one night, when Belinda spoke.

"I say, you've gone very pale, Adele. What's wrong?"

Adele bit her lower lip deliberating whether or not to tell Belinda of her plight. Taking a deep breath and letting it out again, she said, "Oliver specifically told me he was in James's company at the club last night. Oh, Belinda, he's been lying to me for some reason and I have a feeling it's something to do with that young man."

"But surely not? Why would he do something like that?"

"I've no idea...but I intend finding out."

"How will you do that, though?"

"Next time he leaves the house—I'm going to follow him. Will you help me, Belinda?"

"Oh, I don't know if I should get involved, Adele, your husband is my superior at the hospital and a good friend to James."

Adele felt a lump rise in her throat, which she swallowed down as she held back bitter tears of despair. She was so sure Belinda would agree to help her, she'd been planning on asking her friend later, but the tears just spilt out. "Then I shall just have to do this on my own."

"But what will you do?"

"It's probably best you don't find out, Belinda, so you aren't caught up in a sticky situation," Adele replied huffily.

Belinda put her hand on Adele's shoulder, but Adele drew away. She stood and said, "I'm going back inside now, we have a lecture in a few minutes."

"I'll come with you," Belinda said, now sounding downcast herself. It was almost as though an invisible barrier now divided the two and it was all down to her husband and his shifty behaviour.

***

Later that evening after they'd dined and Oliver had said he was off

105

to his gentleman's club once again, Adele went along with it, and as soon as she spied his carriage leaving from outside the door, she put on her hat and jacket and walked outside to the street where she hailed a Hansom cab. She had earlier arranged for one to draw up ready outside, there were several large houses on the tree-lined street and she'd given instructions for it to wait up the road, not to arouse her husband's suspicions.

As she made to get on board, the cabbie opened the door for her, he enquired as he tipped his hat, "Where to Madam?"

"Please can we follow the cab that's just left this house, my husband has forgotten something he urgently needs for a meeting." In her hand she held a sealed letter, just for show, she had earlier written one to pretend she had to give it to her husband. And the beauty of it was, if he caught her, she would pretend she was being taken to find a post box as she'd written to Morag.

"Very well," the cabbie said, closing the door behind her. He took his seat on the back of the cab and pulled away from the kerb, the horses clip-clopping along the cobbled street, and she dreaded what she might discover.

As they reached the end of the road, Adele saw her husband's carriage turn left, then left again and out towards the city, which gave way to an area that was alien to her. There were several pubs where revellers were spilling out onto the street, Chinese laundry houses and various shops packed closely together. Grimy children played in the street, hard-faced women in shabby Linley dresses sat on doorsteps, sleeves rolled up as if ready to deal with their men folk when they returned home. So this was the East End of London. As they passed one shop, she saw the name 'Whitechapel Hardware'. Swallowing, she realised this was the area that Jack the Ripper had struck almost thirty years previously, when he'd savagely murdered five women. The fiend had never been caught, and to this day, people still spoke about him with trepidation. As the cab trundled along, on the left, she noticed a pub bearing the words, *The Ten Bells*. Fear clawed at her throat. That was the pub that some of Jack's victims had drank in. What was her husband doing in an area like this? And beside the pub was Spitalfield's Church, a white beacon of glory in a hell hole of sin.

A few minutes later, Adele watched her husband's carriage draw up outside a small house on a narrow, drab street. The cab driver upon her instruction, parked up down the road, so she could keep watch. If he was curious why she hadn't rushed over to give her husband the letter he 'so badly needed', then he wasn't saying so.

Then her husband got out of the carriage, said something to his driver, and the carriage driver drove off. It was obvious Oliver would be spending some time at the house. She hoped she'd see who he'd come to visit, but instead, he approached the small wooden door and walked straight into the house as if he owned it. Whoever it was he was going to visit, was expecting him, that much was evident. A thought struck her. He had a mistress! No wonder he had no time for her in the bedroom and had been keeping late hours. Maybe the gentleman who had called around was either the woman's husband or even a pimp! Revulsion caused her body to shake, her hands trembled and bitter bile rose in her throat. She needed air, badly. But even more than that, she needed to find out who lived in that house.

This wasn't the time nor place to surprise Oliver, she needed to bide her time and maybe return here another day to find out who lived in that house. It looked very shabby indeed, more like some kind of rough lodging house. What on earth was her husband doing in an area like this? And more importantly, perhaps, why was he lying about his whereabouts?

It was then she broke down and wept. All the confusion and distance between herself and her husband that had occurred since their marriage, came to the fore, and she heaved her shoulders as she let the grief take over, then when she could cry no more, she wiped her eyes on her lace handkerchief.

The cab driver opened the door, "Madame!" he shouted cheerfully as he peered inside, apparently not noticing her distress. "Someone just came up to me on the street, and I don't know if this is true, but the war is over! There's a treaty that's been signed, soon all our men will be back home!" He whooped with delight as Adele sat in the back of the cab, numb and frozen to the spot. She knew she should be pleased it was all coming to an end, after all the men and women had suffered in France and Belgium. Now realising that husbands, fathers and sons would return back home to loved ones again, but for now she was steeped in her own misery and not even the thought of the war being over, could make the pain go away.

Chapter Eleven

All of London appeared to be awash with news that the war was over! People openly celebrated, some making their way to Buckingham Palace or Trafalgar Square fountains. There was dancing in the streets, horns were sounded, streamers thrown and a general sense of liberty and laughter filled the air across the city, but somehow Adele could not be a part of it, as she found herself sinking into a deep depression. Who was this woman her husband was seeing? Was he in contact with her before their marriage? Why couldn't she seem to satisfy his needs? All sorts of thoughts coursed her brain day and night. It wasn't until two days later that Belinda led her out of one of the wards and down a little corridor, into a store room to have a word with her.

"Come on now Adele, it's not like you to be as morose as this. What's happened? Did you find anything out?"

As they stood closed away from the rest of the hospital, in a room stacked floor-to-ceiling with hospital supplies like dressings, bandages, various lotions and potions that smelled strongly of disinfectant, that Adele gave way, she had been holding it to herself for too long.

"It's Oliver, after I spoke to you that day, I followed him when he went out that evening. He'd told me he was off to the club again, but he ended up in Whitechapel."

Belinda's eyes widened as the whites went on show as if horrified by Adele's revelation. "What on earth would he being doing in that hell hole?"

Adele shrugged. "He took a trip to a small, run-down house and didn't even knock the door, just walked inside. Oh, Belinda, he must have a mistress."

Belinda bit her lip, then hugged Adele. "Why do men do these foolish things? He has everything in you, Adele. You're good looking, intelligent, you have a mind of your own..."

"Maybe that's what he doesn't want, a strong woman. Maybe he wants someone to take care of."

"Oh fiddlesticks! He's known all along what you're like. There must be a simple explanation for all of this. Maybe he was visiting a patient."

"Possibly. Though he hasn't made any house calls in a long while as he's so tied up at the hospital with administrative duties. Besides, he didn't have his leather Gladstone bag with him."

"Will you follow him again?"

"No. But I do intend going to that house and knocking the door to see who lives there!"

"Yes, that's a good idea. I just hope it's a little old lady!"

"Me too, though I doubt it will be. I bet it's a beautiful young lady who has fallen on hard times."

"Well, we'll see..."

"We?"

Belinda nodded vigorously. "Yes, next time I'm coming with you. I am sorry I wanted to keep out of it but I can't bear the thought of you walking through Whitechapel alone, it's too dangerous with the sorts that live there."

"Thank you, Belinda. I'd appreciate that. Shall we go tomorrow afternoon when we have a couple of free study hours?"

"Good idea. By the way, isn't it great to see everyone celebrating the end of the war! People seem so carefree."

"Yes, but it's not as simple as that, there is still some fighting going on I'm informed. Fighting continues while peace negotiations are under way..."

"Yes, I suppose we can't expect it all to suddenly stop over night, but I for one, am so glad. My brother Timothy will be coming home soon, he's lucky to get away unscathed."

"Well you say 'unscathed' but in my experience every soldier carries some form of battle scar whether it's outward or inward, my time working with the shell-shocked at Netley told me that."

"Oh Adele, I do admire you so, you have done far more than any other medical student in this hospital. Even performing amputations alone before you even qualified as a surgeon."

"It was a case of having to, Belinda. You don't think of that sort of thing when you're in a war zone."

"But still, you are a true war heroine to me, Adele."

Adele smiled, she certainly didn't feel like any sort of hero compared to what many of those men fighting for their country went through, she felt undeserving of that accolade too.

In the end, Germany and her allies had realised it was no longer possible to win the war, it spoiled their plans for a quick victory when Britain and France counter-attacked. Germany had not been strong enough to continue fighting, especially after America joined the war. It felt to Adele like a very futile war indeed, with a tremendous loss of life. A war she hoped never to see the likes of again during her lifetime.

***

The following afternoon, Adele and Belinda took a motorised cab to Whitechapel and knocked the door of the house where Adele had seen Oliver walk into. Its windows were ingrained and grubby, like all the other houses in the row. Voices arose from inside and it was with a quickening heart-beat, she heard a woman's voice yell out, "Answer the bleedin' door!"

Saddened, she noticed, a blonde-headed lady of about twenty-five years old, open the door. The woman stood there, hand on hip, over her gaudy red dress. Before addressing both women, she shouted behind her, "Hey, there's two sorts here! Ladies by the look of it!"

She heard laughter emanating from within and a young man stood there, in waistcoat, matching trousers, shirt and cravat. His hair was a little long, but otherwise he looked perfectly tidy. "Yes, what can I do for you ladies? Are you here to have your portraits painted?"

Adele and Belinda looked at one another in amusement. "Sorry, we've made a mistake..." Adele mumbled, relieved that her husband had been coming here to have his portrait painted, the man did indeed look like an artist with his wild, Bohemian look. She was just about to step away, when another young man arrived at the doorway— narrowing her eyes, Adele's lungs felt robbed of oxygen as she realised it was the young man who had shown up at her home. Clutching onto Belinda's arm to steady herself, she paused as the young man looked her up and down.

"Oh, it's you!" He said rudely, tossing his tousled dark hair back.

Who were these people? They didn't look the sort that someone of Oliver's standing would associate with?

"You know me?" she asked, when she had finally found her voice.

"Of course I do, dear. You're *his* wife!" He said in an affected manner as the man and woman walked away back into the deep confines of the house. Were they about to be embarrassed by something he said?

"*His*?" She stood with hands on hips. "Yes, I am Oliver's wife.

110

What relevance is it to you? Your name is Wally Tedstone, you called at our house the other evening?"

The man glared at her in such a fashion as to make her feel uncomfortable. "Darling..." he began, rolling the 'r' of the word. "I mean more to your husband than you could ever possibly imagine! And my name is not Wally Tedstone! I just told your butler that to save your husband any embarrassment should the truth come out..."

"Now look here," Adele said, taking a step forward. "I want to know what your relationship with my husband is. I saw you talking to him the other evening in the garden of my home. You looked quite distraught to me."

The young man sniffed. "Yes, you did, but that was business between myself and Ollie."

"*Ollie*? You do sound on familiar terms," she tossed back her head in annoyance. "I've never, ever, heard my husband referred to by that particular name before. Even I don't call my husband by that name!"

"Well, maybe you should, darlin'. Maybe now you realise what I mean to him." He gave her a cold, hard stare which made her feel as though he had the upper hand. A few minutes ago she had just been puzzled about her husband and this man, but now there appeared to be some sort of secret between them she wasn't privy to. And she didn't like that feeling one little bit.

Adele's lower lip quivered as she fought to hold back the tears, desperately trying to think what to say next.

"Come on," Belinda beckoned, "let's leave this dreadful place." Taking Adele's arm, she made to walk way. "You can talk to *Oliver* later."

Adele's eyes were now brimming with tears. "No!" she snapped, withdrawing her arm from Belinda's grasp. "I've come here to discover the truth and I'm not leaving here until the truth finally outs!"

The young man smiled. "I admire your spirit, dear!" He said with a flourish of his hand, he was a very strange person indeed. Why was Oliver so involved with him?

"Look," Adele implored. "What exactly is going on?"

Before the young man had a chance to answer, the woman in the gaudy dress came up behind him and with one arm on the door frame, said, "I should think it's obvious, dearie. Haven't you worked it out yet?"

Adele shook her head, whilst Belinda looked bewildered. "No, I haven't a clue other than to think this man might be blackmailing my husband."

The young man threw back his head and laughed manically. When he had calmed down, his face took on a serious expression. "Ollie and I are lovers, darlin'. We really make sweet music together!"

"No!" Adele said, disbelieving her own ears. She looked at Belinda for confirmation, but her friend just shrugged her shoulders.

"It's true," the woman said. "You husband has been coming here for the last few months. He has a strong desire for young men with a feminine appearance!"

Adele felt a wave of revulsion ebb through her. "You mean to say my husband is in love with this person?"

The woman shrugged. "Well, I don't know if it's love, more like lust, I'd expect, Missus. Look, do you and your friend want to come in and discuss this? Too many nosey parkers around here!" The woman stepped out onto the road raising her voice at two middle-aged women who were passing by, laden down with wicker baskets full of groceries. The women walked off sharpish as if afraid of the woman in the gaudy dress.

Adele hesitated for a moment, then followed the pair inside the low beamed house, with Belinda in close proximity, behind her. The house smelled quite mouldy and damp but otherwise was reasonably clean looking.

The woman, who said her name was Gilda, gestured for them to seat themselves by a large wooden table, she joined them and then asked the young man to sit down.

"What's your real name?" Adele asked him.

"Bernhardt," he said, not quite so cockily now. He pronounced his name slightly different to 'Bernard' which made her wonder if he was foreign maybe, and when she listened carefully, she detected a different brogue.

"Bernhardt," she said, drawing a deep breath and letting it out again, "do you love my husband?"

Without hesitation, he nodded enthusiastically. "Yes, I believe I do."

This was all so strange to Adele, she knew of course that sometimes men and women had sexual relations with their own kind, but the only other person she'd known personally who may have done so, was Moira.

"Exactly how long has the relationship being going on for?" She questioned, gazing into his eyes.

"About six months, I would say."

A stab of pain pierced her heart to think of her husband being so intimate with someone else, whilst he was so distant with her. "So even before he married me?" Adele asked, angrily slapping her hand on the wooden table, which caused a couple of pewter mugs to vibrate.

"Yes, I begged him not to marry you..." Bernhardt explained, his eyes filling with tears, "but Ollie said, it would be a big scandal if people found out about me and him."

"So, he went along with the marriage to me for convenience sake and appearances," Adele said dully. "Sad, he felt the need to do that. It all makes sense now. He's hardly come near me in the bedroom and when he does, is unable to perform his manly duties."

Bernhardt heaved what sounded like a breath of relief. It was evident to Adele this was more than a quick fling on Bernhardt's part, but the revulsion at what her husband had put her through took over, she could no longer carry on living with him and would confront him tonight. How could he have kissed her like that when she returned from The Front? The kiss had felt real, the wedding vows seemed genuine at the time. But what she realised was, he was doing it to save his own skin to cover up a scandal. An eminent doctor involved in homosexuality in the East End of London would not go down at all well with the hospital board and if the newspapers should ever get wind of it, his career would be well and truly over.

***

They arrived back at Mrs Gibson's house for a glass of sherry and a chance to discuss what had just occurred, much of their journey home had been in stunned silence. Mrs Gibson, as if sensing something was up, tactfully kept well out of the way and if she thought it odd both ladies where drinking from her best bottle of sherry, then she wasn't saying so. She just left them to it.

"So, what are you going to do now?" Belinda asked. They were seated in the parlour at opposite ends of a table that was laid with a white lace tablecloth with a vase of fresh yellow roses in the centre. Mrs Gibson did that when meals were over, it made the parlour look pretty. But anything pretty was far away from Adele's mind right now.

"I suppose I need to confront my husband," she said, her hand trembled as she lifted her glass, her mouth was so parched she needed a drink and took a sip of the sherry, which warmed her up inside, somehow comforting her. Now she understood why Oliver had grown so distant toward her, yet to have married her knowing full well there was a side of him that yearned for someone else... None of it made sense and yet all of it made sense. It was a contradiction in terms.

"There's no suppose about it," Belinda said sharply, cutting into Adele's thoughts. "You can't stay with a man who is more interested in other men, it's making a mockery of your recent marriage! And to think I stood there watching you both at the pulpit with tears in my eyes, so happy for you both." Belinda's tone wasn't being helpful, in a sense she seemed to be now making this about her and what she thought of Oliver.

Sadly, Adele drew her eyes, which were transfixed on the roses at the centre of the table, toward her friend. "If you feel like that just as a wedding guest and someone who knows my husband from the hospital as one of your superiors, how do you think I feel as his wife? I thought there was something wrong with me... He hasn't come anywhere near me for weeks, now I know why."

"I'm sorry, Adele," Belinda said softly. "I was just so angry there for you. Of course, you must speak to Oliver, but choose the right time."

"I plan to speak to him following dinner tonight, I can't go around with this churning away at my insides. We have an examination next week to attend and I'll never pass if my mind dwells on this topic."

"Let's hope it's some sort of misunderstanding then."

"Misunderstanding?" Adele straightened her spine. "I hardly think so. Did it sound as if Bernhardt was telling fibs to you?"

"No, to be honest. I felt he was being sincere."

"That's what concerns me, Belinda, that my husband has more feelings for another man than he has for me, his wife."

Belinda patted her friend's hand as Adele wept bitter tears.

***

That evening after making small talk over dinner, and the servants had been dismissed, both husband and wife sat in the drawing room. Oliver stared out of the window, then slowly turned to face Adele. "Your medical exam is next week, is it not?"

She nodded. "Yes."

"I'm not aware of you undertaking any study, Adele, do you think that's wise? You can't expect to sail through these things. You might well have had more experience than the other students put together regarding your work overseas, and in British military hospitals, but what counts is if you can translate your knowledge onto paper."

"I'm well aware of that, Oliver, but thank you for reminding me," she said, stiffly. "I need to have a talk with you."

He glanced at her from the high back chair near the fireplace, the evenings were becoming increasingly chilly of late. "Oh?"

"I need to ask you about Bernhardt..."

Her husband's face visibly paled and he loosened his cravat. "Bernhardt who?" he asked, blinking several times.

"The 'Bernhardt' who was here the other evening, the one who looked most upset."

"Oh, you mean the man who was trying to extort money from me for his pet charity?"

"You can't fob me off any longer. I've been to see him in Whitechapel and he's told me everything. You went along with the 'Wally Tedstone' story but that's not his real name, it's Bernhardt, he told me himself and what you mean to one another!"

Oliver gulped. He was now taking her seriously. "I...I..." He couldn't find the words to reply.

"Your face has gone very white, Oliver. Look, I won't beat around the bush, you're obviously a homosexual who has married me for appearances' sake. No wonder you wouldn't come anywhere near me in the bedroom, except for the odd occasion when you failed dismally. I was beginning to think it was me, but it's you. You cannot get an erect penis for a woman, it has to be a man and a young feminine looking man at that."

She heard a gasp as Oliver began to tremble and then he cried, a deep guttural cry and put his head in his hands. It was all too much for him to bear. In some way, she felt sorrow for his plight and stood, placing a hand on his back as deep racking sobs took over his body.

"It will be all right," she said. "I shall remain with you as long as you will allow me to have my own private life, so I can be fulfilled. I would very much like a child."

He slowly looked up through glassy eyes as if he couldn't believe her suggestion. "You mean you would like to get someone else to father your child?"

She nodded. "Precisely. I've given this a lot of thought and to avoid any scandal for you or myself, I think it could work."

He shook his head. "I really don't think I could share you, Adele...I know it's selfish of me after all I've done, but I really do love you, though not in the way that you wish."

"I think, and I should have realised this before we married, your affections have always been patronly towards me, Oliver. I can see that now, like that time you rescued me from the clutches of Hubert and Moira and the time you paid my rent to Mrs Gibson. You like taking care of me, don't you?" He nodded. "For some reason, I fulfil that role in your life, but your lustful urges have led you to lie with another man or even men..." Which prompted her to ask, "Have there been others, Oliver?"

She could tell by the look in his eyes that of course there had, yet there was not even a whiff of scandal surrounding him that she was aware of. Unless of course any scandal had not reached her own ears, for obvious reasons.

"Yes, there have been a few over the years..."

"Since when?"

"Since I was a young man. I once had a long relationship with an older man, but he sadly passed away and I was celibate for many years, I was grieving for him I think. But then I started frequenting bad places and taking to drink. I'd go out of the area I lived and it was then opportunities began to present themselves to me. I always told myself I could stop at any time, but now I feel I can't. I thought by marrying you, Adele, it would change me. But it didn't."

She stood with hands on hips, her chin jutting out in defiance. "So, I was just an experiment for you?"

"No, no. It wasn't that at all. Like I said, I really do love you, Adele."

"But even if I asked you to stop what you were doing and become a proper husband to me, do you think you could?"

"I could try...I suppose."

"That's not good enough." She hesitated. "I can tell by your very choice of words that you would fail because instead you would have replied, 'I *will* be a proper husband to you,' not 'I *could try*'. I'm afraid that from now on we are going to have to lead very separate lives. To the outside world, we shall appear as though we are a respectable couple and I am having your baby, but *we will know* the truth, Oliver. I shall take a different bed chamber from now on. All I ask is that you keep your lover, Bernhardt, well away from this house!"

He nodded and she realised she had given him a swift stab in his gut, but even that gave her no satisfaction for revenge. "I had considered leaving you and moving back to be with my parents in Wales, but I wouldn't want to disappoint them." She saw the hurt reflected in Oliver's eyes as she said this. "Also I have my career to think of and would like to pass my surgeon's examination. I think it's a situation that could suit us both very well."

She realised she sounded a lot more forceful than was her intention, but she had to put on this facade or otherwise she might crumble.

"Do you love Bernhardt?" She found herself asking.

He shook his head. "No. I have a strong desire for him that I need to quench from time-to-time, but I wouldn't call it love exactly."

"Well, that is your mistake choosing a man who is in love with you, for it will all end in tears, you mark my words."

And she left him with that thought as he sat staring out the window whilst she got herself ready for bed. There were several guest bedrooms in the house she could choose from to sleep in from now on. She chose the one that had an adjoining room for what she intended should become a nursery, for when or if, she got pregnant. But first, she needed to pass those examinations next week.

***

The following morning, her husband was nowhere to be seen at the breakfast table and she wondered if he'd gone out later the evening before and stayed with Bernhardt, but then quite suddenly, as she was sipping her second cup of coffee, he appeared in the doorway, looking breathless with a newspaper tucked under his arm. "I've been thinking things over all night long," he suddenly announced. "And I think we ought to move house!"

She looked at him in astonishment. "Didn't you hear what I said to you last night?"

He looked behind him to ensure none of the servants were around. "Yes, I heard you and you mentioned returning to Wales, that might be a good thing for both of us."

"But that's not going to put pay to your homosexuality, Oliver," she lowered her voice. "You are being quite foolish if you think that. I'm not even saying that what you're doing is a bad thing at all, society condemns it, yes, but you can't help your urges, can you?"

"But I've found a church where the pastor talks to men who have urges, like homosexuality, alcohol, a penchant for prostitutes, etcetera.

He claims he can cure them of their ailments."

Adele scoffed. "I very much doubt that, Oliver. I believe in God, yes, I do, but I feel this is something very much ingrained into your heart and soul."

Quite suddenly, he was beside her on his knees. "Please Adele, give me this one chance to prove I can be cured. I shall pay Bernhardt off to not say anything to anyone, and keep him well away from our door, then I will do my best to become the husband you deserve. I would like to father your child, he or she will want for nothing."

Tears sprung to his eyes and her heart went out to him. Poor Oliver didn't have a family of his own, she was all that he had. Should she give him one last chance to prove himself? Upon her better judgement, she found herself agreeing to this.

"Thank you so much," he said kissing her hand and rising to his feet. "I don't deserve you, Adele. You won't regret it. I shall make an appointment to see the pastor this very day."

Adele sincerely hoped she would not regret the chance she was offering her husband.

Chapter Twelve

Things settled down into a pattern. Adele took her surgeon's examination and was waiting for the result, meanwhile Oliver was doing his best to be a good husband and potential father to a new baby. But it just wasn't happening for them in the bedroom, he just could not get himself into a state of arousal and he was becoming extremely distressed about the situation. Eventually, he agreed it would be best for Adele to take a lover as he did not want to lose her.

"But Oliver, I can't do that now you've promised to be a true and faithful husband to me," she said.

"But you can and you will, my sweet. It's the best way. You can have the child you want so badly and I can have a happy wife. That's all that matters to me right now. To all intents and purposes, I shall be the child's real father."

She deliberated for a moment. "Although it sounds quite simple, it's not. We need to choose a suitable donor who is unmarried and very discreet."

Oliver went into deep thought for a moment, then his eyes brightened like two shiny coals. "By Jove I have it! James Bellingham!" He said with great excitement.

"James?" Adele furrowed her brow. "I don't know about that, he's courting Belinda, isn't he? That wouldn't be right at all."

"They're not exactly courting now Adele, are they? He's only taken her out a couple of times. He's still footloose and fancy free, and best of all, you know and like one another. I am sure he would agree to it."

"Please sit down, Oliver," Adele beckoned.

Her husband's enthusiasm was beginning to wane as he took his usual seat near the fire, it was as if all the stuffing had been knocked out of his insides, and now she was going to tell him something he did not want to hear.

"We'll have no more of this talk. If we are to remain together then we might have to forget about ever having a child. Or maybe we could adopt one. We've had several babies lately at the hospital that needed taking care of. With the men having been away fighting overseas and leaving their girlfriends and wives back home, there have been many unwanted pregnancies. The last thing a soldier needs is to return from the Front Line to find his wife has been unfaithful and there's a reminder of a strange child in her arms. We shall be doing someone a kindness."

"Whatever you think best, m'dear." Oliver twirled his silver-grey moustache and Adele noticed for the first time just how old he was looking of late. Something about her husband's demeanour made her feel he had given up on life. She tried to push everything to the back of her mind and concentrate on her career.

***

James Bellingham was waiting for her when she arrived at the hospital the following day. A sliver of guilt coursed through her veins as she thought back to her husband's suggestion of James fathering her child.

"Hello, Adele," he said, as he stood outside his office in the corridor.

"Hello." A sudden flush to her cheeks arose and she hoped he wouldn't notice.

"I've got good news for you. You performed much better than all the other students in your examination both in the practical and theory—I would like to nominate you for a position here as a permanent house surgeon." He smiled broadly as he looked into her eyes with his own hazel brown ones. She felt her heart flutter.

"Oh, that's good news, but I shall have to discuss this with my husband."

His eyes darkened. "But what's to discuss? You have a glowing career ahead of you if you take the opportunities presented."

She hesitated before replying, "But we had planned to start a family."

"Oh, I see..." He scratched his chin for a moment as if deep in thought. "I honestly don't know what to suggest to you, unless you take some sort of sabbatical."

"Sabbatical?"

"Yes. Go away and have your baby and then when he or she is old enough to be cared for by a nanny or nursemaid, return to the hospital? What do you say?"

"I say it's a good idea."

She thought of little else over the following weeks and months but

120

it just wasn't happening, even though they tried, there was no chance of her becoming pregnant. She decided the best thing they could do was contact an adoption agency. And so, an appointment was made for them both to attend the following month.

One day a couple of weeks later, Adele was sitting in the garden composing a letter to her brother, Thomas. She hadn't seen him since her wedding to Oliver and wondered how he was getting on. She was about to end her letter, when a commotion near the garden gate startled her. Looking up, she noticed the butler running towards the gate himself.

"What on earth is going on, Reeves?" she called out.

"It's the master!" she heard him shout out to one of the livery lads. "He's been injured..."

She dropped her fountain pen on the small table, lifted her skirts and ran toward the gate, where she saw her husband's carriage parked up, with the driver and butler in attendance to their master, inside.

"What's happened?" she shouted, surprising herself by the loud authoritative tone of her voice.

"Your husband was set upon Ma'am," the driver explained. "We were driving through the East End and stopped at a particular street, then a gang of people rushed out and began shaking the carriage and throwing stones. The horses were petrified and reared up, your husband had stood up inside the carriage, and I think the commotion caused him to black out, fall and hit his head. When the gang could see the trouble they'd caused for us, they ran off. Scared, I expect in case the *Old Bill* arrived on the scene."

Adele glanced at Samuel, the livery lad. "Go and fetch Doctor Bellingham from the hospital and when you've done that, help the driver calm and stable the horses," she ordered.

The lad nodded eagerly, and ran off up the street in the direction of the hospital; he was only fourteen-years-old and given a fair bit of responsibility for his age, but was a reliable lad.

Adele clambered inside the carriage to take a look at her husband, who was moaning and mumbling. He had a slight gash on his right temple from which droplets of blood oozed down his face, his clothing appearing to be in disarray.

"Oliver, are you all right?" she asked, her voice full of concern.

He nodded and slowly opened his eyes, then blinked several times. "I'm fine, honestly. It was a bit of a shock that's all."

"Now, you stay there a while, I've sent Samuel to bring James from the hospital to take a look at you. I know he doesn't have any operations today, only paperwork to catch up on, so he should be available, otherwise let's hope the lad will have the sense to fetch someone else."

"He's a good lad," Oliver said, half smiling as his head rested against the carriage window.

"What were you doing in the East End anyhow?" she asked, through narrow slitted eyes.

"It wasn't what you might have been thinking, Adele. I went there as I'd heard of a young lady who was about to give birth to a child. She'd fallen on hard times, I was going to go along and meet the obstetrician there, who told me about her. Obviously, with the thought of bringing a newborn baby back home for you."

"I can't believe what I'm hearing!" Adele stiffened. "That was something we should have discussed with one another. We're not talking about a cute little puppy or kitten here, but a young baby. Anyhow, why were you attacked?"

He shook his head. "Maybe it was a robbery that went wrong, I suppose."

Somehow she didn't quite believe him. "Why go to see that young woman with the sole intention of acquiring a baby when we've made an appointment with the adoption agency?"

He opened his mouth to speak and closed it again. He had no answer. He had to be lying and she needed to find out the truth, but now wasn't the right time.

She remained with her husband until James arrived, breathlessly, as if he had been rushing.

"What's happened?" he asked. "The young lad said your husband had hurt his head?" He stood looking at Adele, his eyes questioning as she now stood outside the carriage whilst her husband remained inside.

"Some people set on him."

James raised a brow and replied, "But this is a fairly decent neighbourhood, who would do such a thing?"

Somehow a feeling of shame overtook Adele about her husband being around the East End, so she quickly changed the subject. "He's inside the carriage, please take a look at him. He says he's fine and I've examined him myself, but I'd prefer your diagnosis."

"And rightly so, Adele. Although you are a fine medical student yourself, you are too close to the situation." He opened the carriage door and got inside, complete with Gladstone bag, returning to Adele's side a couple of minutes later.

"Will he be all right?" She studied James's face for answers.

"Yes, yes. He's just had a shock that's all. He told me that cut on his temple was where someone struck him with a metal poker. It's not too bad, but I prescribe bed rest for at least twenty-four hours with the usual precautions we make for head injuries. Let me know if he suffers any headaches, dizziness or bouts of nausea and vomiting. I've told him he should report the incident to the police, but he's having none of it."

Adele wondered why her husband wouldn't think of reporting such a thing and felt he had something to hide, she would question him about it later when he was fit and well.

She laid her hand on James's forearm. "Thanks for coming," she said appreciatively.

He smiled. "It's all in a day's work. I'd get a couple of the servants to help him inside the house and put him to bed. He can have a drop of brandy for medicinal purposes, not too much mind you, and a light diet. A little fresh air in the garden tomorrow wouldn't go amiss either, but keep him away from the Club until he gets his confidence back. This will have knocked the stuffing out of him, I'm sure," he said lowering his voice.

She was sure it had. "Thank you, James."

"I'll call around tomorrow to see how the old boy is doing," he smiled a smile that went straight to her heart. Oh, why hadn't she waited for him instead of running into Oliver's arms when she returned to London?

She watched him leave the property, standing erect in his long coat and wearing his bowler hat at a jaunty angle. Every inch the gentleman, she let out a long sigh and turned her attentions back towards her husband.

***

The following day, as she sat in the garden with Oliver, under a large oak tree, she turned to him and asked, "Oliver, what were you really doing over at the East End again?"

He peered over his newspaper. "I've already told you, I was summoned to the home of a young, pregnant woman, who was ready to give birth."

She shook her head sadly. "Look, you and I know the people living in the Whitechapel area hardly have a farthing to rub together, why would they summon any doctors from the hospital? They see to themselves and that includes giving birth. How would the obstetrician have even known about this young lady you mention?"

His face reddened, and he appeared to avoid eye contact with her. "I really don't know," he said, returning to his newspaper and turning the page, as if hoping she would drop the subject, but she wasn't prepared to do so.

"I know you're lying!" she spat out the words, suddenly surprising herself with the vehemence of her own tone of voice. "I will find out— I shall visit the area myself tomorrow."

Oliver set down his newspaper. "No, you will not. I forbid it!"

"You can't stop me!" She shouted at him and standing, turned towards the house. James was due to visit this afternoon to check on Oliver's progress and she needed to calm down. A glass of lemonade and a moment alone was needed to help.

She had just set down her glass and was feeling a little better when there was a knock at the door, the butler allowed James into the hallway.

Adele rose to her feet to greet him.

"How's the patient?" James asked.

"He's fine," Adele replied, then she waited until the butler had departed.

"What's wrong?" James asked, searching her eyes as if sensing something were amiss.

"It's Oliver. I know he's lying to me, James. He claims he was over the East End yesterday when he was clobbered as he was going to the home of a young pregnant woman. He told me an obstetrician had informed him about a young woman who was about to give birth, who was looking for a home for her baby so that he could give me the child, but I don't believe him."

James shook his head. "I have to admit it does sound improbable. And why would he try to get a child for you, unless he can't father one himself?" His eyes widened as if he was just realising that were the case.

"More to the point and I didn't want to tell you this..." she lowered her voice, "he was going over to the Whitechapel area quite regularly, making out he was going to the Club."

"But he wasn't?"

She shook her head. "No, I followed him one day, he walked straight into a house not far from the Ten Bells pub at Spitalfields. The next day, I knocked the door there and discovered the truth. It's horrendous, James. I haven't told anyone of this, only Belinda knows as she was with me at the time."

"Knows of what?"

Tears filled her eyes as James lifted her chin with his thumb and forefinger to gaze into them. "I discovered why my husband had been going there regularly..."

"Another woman?"

She shook her head. "It's another *man*. A young man at that, they were having a relationship with one another. Please don't tell anyone. Oliver might be forced to leave the hospital if it were discovered."

James swallowed hard. "I can hardly believe what I'm hearing from you, Adele, surely there must be some mistake? He would never have married you if he were like that, surely?"

She shook her head. "Look, come with me into the drawing room, I don't want anyone to hear what I have to say."

He followed her, where she closed the door behind them and related the whole sorry tale to him.

He came over to where she sat and patted her hand. "You poor poppet. You can't stay here, Adele. You need to get away. You can stay at my place should you wish."

She shook her head. "No, thank you. It's ever so kind of you, but people would talk. Anyhow, Oliver has now ended the affair."

"Are you sure of that?"

"Yes. But I do believe he's lying about his reason for going to the East End yesterday."

"Then you have got to find out the truth for your own sanity, but the very reason he's not telling you indicates there's a flaw in your relationship, I'm sad to say." He gently touched her face, as she gazed out of the French windows to see her husband still seated beneath the tree staring in the distance. What was he thinking of? It obviously wasn't her, was it?

James gently wiped away a tear with his thumb that had coursed down her cheek.

"Look," he said softly, "far be it for me to come between a husband and wife, but if he won't tell you, I should threaten to leave him."

"Oh, I couldn't do that James. I need to ask you a favour."

"Ask away..."

"Would you come with me if I visit the young man's house? His name is Bernhardt."

"Very well. I should not want to see you go there unaccompanied, and there are very few people you can trust with that information. I would take my car, but driving through that area and parking it up, I would probably return to a wreck without wheels!"

"We could take one of our carriages. We were going to buy an automobile ourselves, but although Oliver is capable of driving, he refuses to do so around London, which makes me wonder if he squandered a lot of money on that young man and is using it as an excuse as he can't afford one."

James rubbed his chin. "That is entirely possible I suppose. Anyhow, how about we go tomorrow?" She nodded, pleased she would have company for the journey to the East End. "Now I had better go and see how the patient is. No symptoms from him?"

"No, none at all," she smiled. She really was pleased her husband was all right physically, but emotionally was another matter altogether.

Chapter Thirteen

The following afternoon, James Bellingham accompanied Adele to Whitechapel. Her heart skipped a beat as the coach clattered across the cobbles as they passed The Ten Bells pub and the lovely white church with its tall spire opposite Spitalfield's market. Finally, they reached the house she'd visited previously.

"Will you come with me?" She asked James.

Without hesitation, he replied, "Of course I will, Adele. I would never allow you to go there alone." She could tell by his tender look and soft gentle voice, that he really cared for her. If only things had worked out differently between them. Maybe if she'd remained in France or he'd returned home sooner, they would be together as a couple now. It was no use dwelling on what might have been, she chastised herself. Then taking a deep breath, she prepared herself for what felt akin to stepping into the lion's den. She feared what she was about to discover.

James assisted Adele down from the coach, then he tipped the cabbie and asking him to return in one hour's time. Instead of taking her husband's cab, James had insisted on flagging one down, as he didn't want to arouse her husband's suspicion, nor the servants. Mrs Charlton, the housekeeper, was very astute and would have wondered where they were both off to, so maybe it was better that way.

Adele steeled a breath as she watched James knock on the shabby front door. It was a while before anyone answered and when they did, it was the woman in the gaudy dress, who she met the first time.

"Oh, it's you, is it?" she said sharply.

"Pardon?" Adele blinked several times. Why did the woman look so displeased to see her? They had parted on civil terms.

"Well, you've got a right nerve coming here after all that has happened and 'im not yet cold in his grave!"

"Who's died?" James asked, butting in.

"Why Bernhardt of course, he broke his 'eart over your 'usband, Missus!"

"Sorry, I don't understand," Adele said, standing there playing with the strap of her bag, something she did when she was nervous.

"'Ere you better come inside before those nosey blighters around these parts 'ears you."

They followed her inside the musty building and sat at the kitchen table.

"What happened to Bernhardt?" James asked.

Adele just wasn't taking it in, expecting the young man to appear at any given moment like he had done on that previous occasion.

"Well, once your husband gave him up, Missus," the woman said, addressing Adele and ignoring James, "he broke 'is heart, he did. Took to the drink, see. Was over the Ten Bells, day and night when he could afford it. Pining he was like a puppy dog. Wasting away..."

A shard of severe guilt sliced through Adele. This was her fault—the woman was saying in a round about way. If she hadn't come here meddling and putting a stop to what was going on, they very well might not be having this conversation at all.

"And what happened then?" James asked.

The woman, still looking directly at Adele said, "Well, he was clean out of money, see. Didn't make much from those paintings of 'is and didn't want to pick any blokes up. He tried to see your 'usband, but Ollie as Bernhardt called him, refused to see him one night. So he walked to the Thames and threw himself in. 'is body has never been found to this day...Tragic it was..." She sniffed and sobbed into the sleeve of her dress, resting her head on the table.

"So, my husband knew of his death?"

"Yes, when he called here to see him yesterday afternoon, it was more than meself and the other boarders and friends of Bernhardt could take, so we played havoc with him, shaking the carriage and one man, threatened to punch his lights out! But of course, we didn't in the end. He's not as young as he was, so I told them all to stop it as I like the man meself, but I was so angry about what happened to me dear friend. Your 'usband gave us some guilt money before he left to ease his conscience, I expect."

Adele had felt like compensating the woman herself and had her hand on her bag, but James shook his head to warn her not to. "Thank you for telling me about this," Adele said flatly. "My husband shall not be visiting these parts anymore and I should be most grateful if you do not tell anyone of what's gone on here."

The woman, narrowed her eyes to slits, her red-haired curls bouncing on her head as if she disliked the fact her performance was now forced to come to an end when she felt she had so much more to say. Adele sensed she was becoming angry and suspicious. "It ain't me you need to be worrying about dearie, it's some of the others. They know the identity of your 'usband. Not 'is name as such as dear Bernhardt was the sole of discretion, but the fact the man is a doctor and if they go to the *Star* or some other newspaper, he wants to watch out. Now then, I can help stop them doing that for a small fee..." She held out her grimy hand. Her fingernails were caked with filth.

"How much do you want to keep people quiet?" Adele asked.

"I think a few sovereigns should do it," the woman replied without any apparent qualms.

James shook his head sadly, but Adele dismissed his opinion and handed the woman five sovereigns, it was all that she had.

"A pleasure doing business with yer Missus, and if you want anything, anything at all, yer know where to come. And you too, Sir. If you want a nice buxom lass to sit on yer knee or to go upstairs with you, well it can be arranged..."

"Er no, thanks," James said respectfully, "I think I'll pass, not my cup of tea and all that."

When they'd departed and found themselves in the grimy street outside, Adele shook with emotion as James cradled her to him. "Come on, let's get out of here, Adele. You've had another nasty shock. You shouldn't have given that woman any money though, as if she finds out who you are and where you live, she might well try to claim more. We've got to put a stop to all of this, if it gets into the newspapers, they'll have a field day. The hospital board will haul Oliver over the coals for it."

"You are right, James, it was foolish of me. I just felt sorry for Gilda and her plight at losing her friend."

"You're too nice you are. Really. Look there's the cab parked up the road, let's get out of here, it's most eerie." They left the area and went to find a tea room near the hospital, where they could sit and relax and discuss the next course of action.

"The thing is Adele..." James said, taking a bite from a small fancy cake and then chewing and swallowing, "what are you going to do now? You can't possibly stay with a man who has lied to you like that? As much as I respect Oliver as a being a first class doctor and colleague, I do not hold with his treatment of you. You deserve so much more."

She swallowed hard, knowing he was absolutely right. Taking her lace handkerchief, she dabbed the crumbs of the cake she'd been eating, away from her lips with a lace handkerchief, and then took a sip of tea before replying, "I can't abandon my husband now in his time of need, he's not getting any younger, but at least I understand now why he was so morose. We have got to protect him, James."

"Protect him from what exactly?" James said, quirking a brow.

"From any scandal that he might have to endure."

"I really don't see how we can do that, though. Those newspapers are quite fierce with their headlines if they get a mere whiff of anything untoward."

At that point, a woman entered the tea room wearing a cloche style hat, the hem of her dress being a little shorter than was usual, which turned the men's heads. Her hair was short and in the new shingle style. It gave Adele an idea, she was going to revamp her image, it might do her the power of good. The only person she'd heard of doing this before, was the actress and dancer, Irene Castle, who had lobbed off her locks as a matter of convenience and her hairstyle had become known as 'The Castle Bob'. It was such a daring thing to do when most women wore their hair long and loose or pinned up on top of their heads.

People in the tea room were beginning to stare and gossip about the woman, who Adele thought looked quite marvellous. Her appearance was so striking and stylish.

Rising from her chair, Adele neared the lady, who had a beautiful fragrance about her and wore a bright red lipstick on her lips, her eyes were heavily lidded with a smoky eye shadow, she looked every inch a star. "Excuse me for asking you," Adele began, "but I do love your hairstyle. Where did you get it styled?"

The woman turned toward Adele and smiled broadly. "I've just returned from Paris and I got it styled there. I couldn't find anywhere around here that would style it for me, most hairdressers are refusing to do this style."

"Is that where you got your beautiful perfume from too, Paris?" Adele asked.

The woman nodded. "Yes, I have to admit it takes some guts to wear this hairstyle. Most of the women I encounter give me the evil eye, but their menfolk, in general, seem to admire it, though there are a few who have told me women should keep their hair long."

Adele smiled. "Good for you," she said, before returning to her seat.

"What did you say to that lady?" James asked.

"Oh I was admiring her hair style, I should very much like that style myself, it would be far more practical for me being a doctor, and I adore the style. The only other person I knew with a short style was Moira, but we all knew where her leanings were and she was more like one of the men anyhow."

"Where would you go to get it styled, though?"

Adele looked thoughtful for a moment. "That lady had hers styled in Paris, but as she told me it's difficult to get a lady's hairdresser to style it, I might ask Oliver's barber, he comes to the house once a month."

James chuckled. "Adele, you're the only lady I know who would think of doing something like that. But to get back to a serious subject...What are you going to do about Oliver?"

"Nothing at all. At least Bernhardt is no longer a threat to our marriage. I'm sorry he's dead and all that, but I shall no longer have to worry about my husband travelling to Whitechapel."

"That might be so, but doesn't it concern you that he lied to you and went there in the first place? Going behind your back?"

"Yes, of course, it does, but I can at last put all that behind me."

James shook his head as if somehow he doubted it.

Chapter Fourteen

When Adele returned home, Oliver was sitting in the high-backed, winged, Queen Anne chair, facing the window, staring unseeingly out of it. He didn't even turn his head as she approached. His mind was elsewhere, that much was evident. But where? What was he thinking? She longed to know but maybe at the same time, she didn't want to know either.

"Evening meal will be ready shortly, Mrs Charlton just informed me!" Adele announced.

"I don't think I could eat anything..." he said in barely a whisper, as he remained staring out of the window. He didn't even see her anymore, she might just as well be a part of the furniture.

"Try some soup at least, it's cream of mushroom, nothing too heavy."

"Very well." Slowly he turned his head. "You've cut your hair!" He exclaimed.

"Yes, do you like it? Obviously, I didn't cut it myself. I asked around most of the hairdressers in the area, but none of those could cut a shingled bob, so I went to the barbers instead and then asked Milly to wave it for me with the curling irons. She's ever so good that young girl. I know she helps Mrs Charlton in the kitchen, but I really think we could give her some more responsibility. In fact..."

"You never even asked my permission..." Oliver said sadly.

"Do I really need your permission, though? I am a doctor like yourself, I can do everything you can do. In any case, there are certain things you didn't ask my permission for."

His hands gripped the sides of his armchair, the knuckles whitening as she stood directly in front of him, towering over him. "Such as?"

"Such as taking our coach into the East End of London on more than one occasion."

His eyes widened, showing the whites of his eyes as his forehead beaded perspiration. She was making him feel very uncomfortable indeed without really saying much at all, just alluding to things.

"Very well, as you wish. You ladies are becoming most liberated these days thanks to those Suffragettes. Next thing, you'll be telling me

132

you're joining them."

"No, not at the moment. I admire some of the things they do to make the voices of women heard, but some of their practices are quite shocking. I don't uphold violence or acts of aggression." She patted her hair, liking the way it felt a lot lighter now that it was cut.

"I suppose I'll get used to it," he said, in a resigned fashion.

"I wanted it styled for Morag and Donald's wedding next week. I know I've asked you previously to accompany me and you thought you had a lot on that day, but has that now changed?"

He frowned and shook his head. "No, I think it would be best if you took someone else along with you, maybe Belinda or even James."

Her heart sank. "But I wanted you to accompany me. There's almost a week to go, you'll be back on your feet by then."

"Sorry, I just don't want to go."

"Is it because you miss Bernhardt so very much!" She spat out the words and they were out of her mouth before she intended.

He stared at her with tears in his eyes, trembling all over, telling her all she needed to know. She couldn't even compete with a dead person. James was absolutely correct, she needed to get out of here. And fast.

That evening she packed a bag and took herself off to a nearby hotel. She couldn't afford to stay there for too long, she'd have to make other arrangements. Oliver watched her leave without a murmur, he didn't even beg her to stay, which made her departure all the easier.

***

At the hotel she felt desolate and so alone, wishing she was back in France. At least there she was needed and treated with the utmost respect.

"Pull yourself together, Adele!" she said firmly. She got up from the bed and washed and changed for dinner.

She was dining alone in the packed restaurant, when she looked up and saw a stranger stood in front of her. "Excuse me, Madame, but would you mind if I share this table? The restaurant is very busy this evening." He was astonishingly handsome, dark-haired with a thin twirled moustache, she guessed he was around her age. His French accent made her want to melt.

She looked at him, her mouth dry for a moment, so she took a sip of water, which she'd poured from a glass carafe. Was it normal for strange men to ask ladies could they sit at their table on the Continent? She guessed maybe it was. Gazing around the room, she could see no other spare seats, so gestured for him to be seated. He took a seat opposite her. "*Merci.* My name is Jean Pierre," he said with a flourish. "I am indebted to you, Madame, I need to dine early as I have an appointment later on this evening."

"Oh?" She blinked several times.

"Yes, I am a silk trader from France. Now the war is over, I am free to travel back and forth between London and Lyon..."

At that point, the waiter arrived to take his order and when he'd departed, Jean Pierre looked directly at Adele and asked, "So, what is a beautiful, stylish lady, like yourself doing here alone?"

She thought it quite forward of him to ask such a personal question and found herself colouring up, then her formal doctor side kicked in. "I'm just staying here for a night or two, but shall be moving on," she replied, hoping that would be the end of his questioning.

"Oh I see...then maybe you would be prepared to join me tomorrow for a tour of the city?"

She almost choked on her glass of water. "Mr. Pierre, I am a married woman..." she said with a note of mischief in her voice.

He glanced at her hand and took in the gold band on her fourth finger of the left hand. "There was no harm intended, believe me, *ma cherie...* It's just now the war is over, I thought I would have time for some sightseeing. I never seem to get the chance when I am in London. It's always, how you say...work, work, work! But I have my final meeting tonight with a prospective buyer, then I have two days to tour the city."

Adele thought for a moment, what would be the harm in her having some fun for a change? She wasn't due back at work until the day after tomorrow. "Very well, Mr. Pierre, I shall accompany you tomorrow for a tour of the city, I would like to see it myself. But I need to return to work the second day."

His left eyebrow lifted in puzzlement. "You work, Madame? But what do you do, someone of your refinement?"

"I am a medical student. I am in my third year of training. I was out in France myself for some time and also worked at a casualty clearing station in Belgium, under the wing of an eminent surgeon from the Royal Free Hospital."

"*Zut alors*! This is the first time I have ever met a female doctor. And to think you have worked in a war zone too! What does your husband think of you? Does he see you as a heroine, because I think you are one, so brave yet so gentile."

She hesitated a moment before replying, "Well I wasn't married to my husband whilst I served in France and Belgium, but to be honest, I have left him this very evening."

Jean Pierre studied her for a while before asking, "Is that why you look so sad, *ma cherie?*"

"Maybe. I didn't realise I looked sad, but I have to admit I am full of regret for what should have been. You see, I had two suitors, but chose the wrong one. My husband is a lot older than myself."

"You mean you should have chosen the younger one, the surgeon?"

Startled and feeling a trifle hot, Adele asked, "But how did you realise?"

Jean tapped the side of his nose with his index finger. "I cannot tell you." Then he chuckled. "In all seriousness, it was the way you spoke of him."

"How so?"

"Full of pride and passion."

She had not realised she'd spoken of him in that way, but Jean Pierre was correct. At that point, the waiter returned with soup for Adele and *Escargot* for Jean Pierre.

"I have often wondered how you French can eat snails and frogs' legs," she tittered.

"And I have often wondered how you English eat things like, Spotted Dick and Toad in the Hole!" Jean laughed.

"Touché," she nodded and smiled.

They finished their meals and then Jean Pierre ordered a bottle of *Sauvignon blanc* wine as they sat chatting for a while, easy in one another's company. This was most daring for Adele to spend time with a stranger but she enjoyed his tales of living in Lyon and his stories about his work. It was highly liberating after all that Oliver had put her through of late. By the time she was ready for bed, she found herself looking forward to exploring the city tomorrow with Jean Pierre.

The following morning, the French man did not show for breakfast which seemed odd as they were supposed to take an omnibus to visit a museum, view St Paul's Cathedral, and had intended having lunch and a walk by the Thames. Jean Pierre had even mentioned maybe they could take to the water and go for a boat trip too, something she hadn't done since she was a young child living in London with her parents. Indeed, she had been so busy this past year or so serving overseas and then there were her marriage and studies, she'd had little time to view the area she dwelled in.

Adele finished her tea and toast and summoned one of the waiters to the table. "Do you remember a French man dining here, last night?"

He nodded vigorously. "Yes, Madame."

"Have you seen him this morning? Has he dined as yet?"

"No, Madame. I haven't seen him today. Have you a message you'd like to send him?"

She wiped away some invisible crumbs from her lips with her napkin, then set it down. "Yes, please. Would you tell him I shall be making my way to the museum and St. Paul's as planned, then to the Thames, should he wish to join me later."

"Very well, Madame." The waiter cleared her table as she stood to leave and she hoped he'd remember to pass on her message. Whatever, if she went out today, it would do her some good and take her mind off things, whether Jean Pierre decided to put in an appearance or not. Since the war had ended, London seemed to be full of a jovial spirit. Everywhere she looked, people had a spring in their step. The shops were nicely decorated with holly and other festive wares in preparation for Christmas and there was a definite nip in the air, but no snow as yet had fallen.

After strolling around the museum and visiting the Egyptian artefacts section, followed by the art gallery, she stopped to gaze at one painting of the Madonna and Child. It brought a tear to her eye to realise that motherhood might never happen for her. She was dabbing away at her eyes, when a male voice said, "Please allow me," turning, she saw Jean Pierre stood there, looking even more handsome as the morning sun filtered through the large museum windows. He took his silk handkerchief from his pocket and dabbed at her eyes. She didn't know whether to laugh or cry but found herself smiling at his very kind gesture.

"I'm sorry, Adele...I slept in too long this morning after that bottle of wine we consumed last night, by the time I made it to breakfast, you had already left but the waiter told me where you were, so I had a quick cup of coffee and a croissant, and here I am!" He beamed at her, apparently pleased to have found her.

She had never been so happy to see someone in all her life, she had felt so alone and desolate for a moment there.

"But why were you crying?" Jean Pierre asked, gazing into her eyes.

"For a moment when I studied that painting, I realised I might never have a child of my own..."

"Oh, *ma cherie*, surely that can't be so, you are a very attractive lady indeed. You husband is a very silly man if you ask me." She allowed him to take her hand and lead her outside into the winter sunshine.

Later, they visited St. Paul's Cathedral which she found breathtakingly beautiful with its English Baroque style interior. Then they walked towards the Thames. There was a large boat waiting to leave which served luncheon on board. Jean Pierre persuaded her to join him, even though she had earlier lost her appetite, it now returned as she gazed at the familiar sites of the Houses of Parliament and other well-known landmarks as they cruised on by. They were seated near the window and served Eggs Benedict as a starter, followed by a roast beef dinner with all the trimmings, finally finishing with a sherry trifle and plenty of top-ups to their coffee cups. Afterwards, Jean Pierre ordered a cognac each, which arrived in a large bulb-shaped glass. Adele had never tasted it before but it was just what she needed as it warmed her to the core on such a crisp, cold day.

She glanced across the table and caught him gazing at her. "*Ma cherie*, the light makes you look so beautiful, like a delicate piece of porcelain...a true English rose..."

"Now, that's where you're wrong," she laughed. "I really consider myself Welsh, even though I was born in London! My parents are both Welsh and we lived here until I was around ten-years-old, but then moved back to Merthyr Tydfil."

He frowned momentarily. "Then why did you choose to return to London, are your family here now?"

"Well, yes and no. My siblings live here, they're a lot older than myself. You see my father was married to another lady many years ago. She had a delicate constitution and was found drowned in the river."

"Oh, Adele, that is most sad. So later he met and married your mother and then you were born?"

"Precisely. My parents are still in Merthyr Tydfil. I returned to London to undertake my doctor's training. It hasn't been at all easy for women to train, but thankfully, it's getting easier. The male students though were a right pain when I started training, but since I've shown them what I'm capable of, they now seem to hold me in high regard."

"You mean they respect you as you have worked as a doctor on the Front Line in Belgium and France?"

"Exactly so." She bit her lip.

"What is it you are not telling me, Adele?"

Tears filled her eyes. "Oh, Jean Pierre, I haven't really told anyone about my feelings..."

"You British and your 'stiff upper lips'," he chuckled, as he took her hand in his. "Go on, you may tell me, you are safe to do so."

"It's just some of the sights I saw out there. Men with half their stomachs blown away, young men crying for their mothers, soldiers losing limbs due to trench foot and shrapnel injuries. Even soldiers who'd been gassed, gasping for breath. It was horrendous."

"But as you were only in training, you would not have had to deal with all that death and destruction on your own, surely?"

"No, not at first, but then there were many times when I was the only surgeon available. The first time I was left alone to deal with things and I had to instruct the nurses, I trembled from top-to-toe, I tell you I felt like deserting my post. But something kept me rooted to the spot. The hardest thing was that I had to prioritise and decide quite often who deserved to live and who to die."

"That must have been dreadful for you, poor Adele."

"It was. But I accept it had to be done. I chose those that I felt had the best chance of survival over those that I felt were either too badly injured or maybe too old to recover, or whatever."

"Not an easy decision, I'm sure." He patted her hand. "How about a walk on deck to blow those cobwebs away?"

She smiled and nodded, then swallowed a large lump in her throat. Talking about things helped her and she realised for the first time that Jean Pierre was much easier to talk to than her own husband had been. In the end, he'd grown very distant towards her, but in retrospect, now she understood why. Her husband was now grieving for someone who had loved him wholeheartedly. It was a lifestyle he yearned to embrace but was something forbidden by society. She didn't feel any bitterness towards Oliver, his heart was in the right place, but he wasn't able to live the life he wanted, and she realised how very hard that must have been for him to contend with.

***

After spending several hours in Jean Pierre's company, Adele realised it was time to say goodbye. She needed to find somewhere permanent to stay and the next day she would be returning to the hospital to work. They were both stood outside her hotel room.

"It has been such a pleasure meeting with you, Adele," Jean Pierre said, taking her hand and planting a kiss upon it. That saying, 'Parting is such sweet sorrow' felt true for Adele on this occasion. "I hope we shall be able to meet again next time I'm in London. Though I won't have an address to contact you?" He said, with a look of concern furrowing his brow.

"You could send a letter to The Royal Free Hospital addressed to Adele Worthington. That's my married name, I was previously an Owen."

"Whatever you wish, Adele."

For a moment, she wondered why he didn't give her his address. Maybe he was married and she'd never get to meet him again. All the best ones usually were. It was a shame he wasn't staying long enough as she could have taken him with her to Morag's wedding. James had said he'd accompany her, but now that she'd left her husband, she didn't want to cause trouble between the two friends even though it had been her husband's suggestion to take James along in the first place. It had grieved her at the time that Oliver wouldn't go with her, she felt she wasn't a part of a couple anymore, if indeed, she ever was.

Jean Pierre kissed her gently on the cheek and she stood watching him walking off down the corridor, leaving her wondering if she'd ever see him again.

***

The following day, Adele wondered if she'd run into Oliver that day at the hospital but he was nowhere to be seen. Mr. Woodrow-Smythe had asked to see her in his office. Oh dear, what was up now? Had he heard about her split from Oliver? When she got there he asked her to be seated and then his face broke out into a huge smile, which was very unusual for him as usually he looked so dour or expressionless even.

"I've some excellent news for you, Adele..." he announced. "The hospital has received word that you are to be awarded the British War Medal."

"Me?" she blinked furiously. "What have I done to deserve this?"

"Yourself and James Bellingham have been chosen from this hospital along with nursing staff and medical orderlies who went out as a team to France. You ask what you did? You saved many, many lives out there, and showed great courage in that casualty clearing station. Not only that, but for your work with shell-shocked soldiers both in France and here in Britain at Netley."

She shrugged her shoulders. "I was only doing my job, honestly."

Mr. Woodrow-Smythe smiled kindly at her. "You know when you first came to the hospital, Adele, I will admit I wasn't your greatest fan. You ruffled quite a few feathers but you have more than proved yourself here. You've held your own and that's what's impressed me. You deserve that medal. I've put it to the board and a ceremony will be held here next month with a special luncheon for you all."

Adele felt her face grow hot and she hoped she didn't look too red. "T...Thank you," she stammered. She didn't often feel comfortable in the limelight but nevertheless, she had to be gracious about it and was pleased for James and everyone else and of course, her family would be thrilled. "Are we allowed to invite anyone to the ceremony?" she asked hopefully.

"Well isn't Oliver coming along?" Mr. Woodrow-Smythe asked, as he searched her eyes for answers.

"No. We've separated." There, she'd said the words she'd been dreading to say and it didn't feel at all too bad.

"Oh, I see. Far be it for me to interfere, but maybe it's teething troubles you haven't been married for long."

"It's more than that I'm afraid. I don't see us reconciling anytime soon."

He nodded. "I understand. No worries, the hospital board shall support the two of you as you are both assets to this hospital."

She began feeling uncomfortable and dreaded the thought of being asked any further questions about her marriage, so took it as an opportunity to escape. "Thank you. I need to get to the ward now."

He stood to show her to the door. "In light of what you've told me, you can either invite your mother and father, or a friend or other relative, Adele."

She nodded and smiled, deciding not to invite her parents as they might ask too many questions about Oliver. Instead, she decided to invite her brother Tom, as he'd served in France and Belgium himself and of course, was living in London.

There was no sign of James Bellingham on the ward that afternoon, puzzled she carried on working, another doctor had provided cover. By the end of her shift, after several medical emergencies had arrived on the ward, Adele felt ready to drop and was about to leave when James himself arrived on the ward huffing and puffing.

"What's going on, James?" Adele asked pointedly.

"It's your husband..." he panted. "I've just been around to see him, he's in a bad way, crying and upset, he's missing you, Adele."

"I'm afraid it's not me he's missing, James, I told you all this the other night."

"Maybe, but he told me he missed you badly and was sorry for any upset incurred."

She shook her head. "How did you find out anyhow?"

"That livery lad, Samuel, came to look for me. Said he'd found Oliver collapsed in a heap, he'd been drinking whisky by the look of it. I found someone to cover here for a few hours and went to see him. I got Mrs Charlton to give him lots of water as he must have been so dehydrated after the whisky and we put him to bed. I'm not telling you that you ought to return to him as I know just how hurt you are, dear Adele. But please just call around some time to see him."

"Very well. But he is no longer my husband. I am going to get the marriage annulled as it was never properly consummated in the first place. He led me a merry little dance."

James nodded as if he understood all too well. "If you need me to accompany you, just say so."

"I will, that's a good idea as I should not be too comfortable going there alone..." she paused for a moment. "By the way, what do you think about the fact we are to be presented with the British War Medal?"

He smiled. "Yes, I was very pleased about that, not so much for myself, but for you, Adele. We really do have something to celebrate, though."

"Well before that time we have a wedding to attend. Morag and Donald's wedding is in a couple of days, are you still willing to accompany me?"

"For sure, I'm really looking forward to it. Have you solved your accommodation problem yet? You know I'd always put you up at my place." He looked at her expectantly as if hoping she'd say, yes.

She nodded. "It's very kind of you, James, but I called to see Mrs Gibson this morning. She's given me my old room back now that Belinda's moving out. I'll have to pay more rent as I don't wish to share, don't think I'd find another roommate like Belinda."

James chuckled for a moment. Then his face took on a serious expression. "I had no idea that Belinda was leaving?"

"Yes, she's going to share with someone else a little nearer the hospital. She said if she'd known I'd be back, she wouldn't have left in the first place as she really likes Mrs Gibson and our landlady is very fond of her too. I thought you'd have known?"

"I haven't seen Belinda for a couple of weeks, she seems too wrapped up with the Suffragette Movement at the moment and I'm sorry to say this, but it's affecting her work here at the hospital."

"Maybe someone needs to have a word with her, it would be a pity if her studies were affected by it."

James nodded. "Yes, I'll have a word with her myself tomorrow."

So, Belinda and James were not courting one another as she'd previously thought. Maybe there was hope on the horizon after all.

Chapter Fifteen

Adele wore a new teal silk dress for Morag and Donald's wedding, with a sheer chiffon wrap and a corsage of white roses, which always reminded her of her grandmother back home in Wales.

When James turned up to meet her, looking devilishly handsome in a dark blue-grey suit, silver cravat and top hat, her heart almost melted. He'd hired a driver to take them there in style.

"My dear, you do look lovely!" He enthused, tipping a wink to Mrs Gibson, who stood by with tears in her eyes.

"That husband of yours doesn't know what he's missing Adele," she said. "I've always admired the good doctor as you know, but he's gone down in my estimations lately."

Adele turned in the passageway to confront Mrs Gibson. "Oh, you mustn't say that, Edna. He's still a good man. I've been to see him and he's truly sorry how things worked out between us."

Edna smiled a thin watery smile, but Adele knew that the woman sensed something was up on Oliver's part, though of course, she hadn't filled the woman in on any of the details. "Never you mind, Adele, you have a lovely day with your new beau," Edna said, patting Adele gently on the shoulder.

"James is certainly not my new beau, are you James?" Adele asked incredulously.

"Er no, but if you'd like me to be?" He joked, making Edna giggle. It was as if they were both in on some private joke Adele was not a part of, ordinarily she might find something like that amusing but it was too close to home, Oliver was hurting badly inside and she felt there wasn't a thing she could do about it.

They arrived at the countrified church, which was set out of the way behind a low stone wall, on top of a hill that had the most astonishing view over the area. "Surely, this can't be it?" Adele said blinking, looking around. There was hardly a sound, which seemed so strange after being in London.

"Yes, it is from directions given, seems we are the first to arrive," James announced, obviously pleased with his punctuality after the drive from the big city. He tapped the side of the car, which was a

Rover 12. "Nice work, Jenks," he said to the chauffeur. "If you can hang around until the church ceremony is over, then transport us to the reception, which I believe is only about a mile away, then leave us for a few hours and come back to collect us."

Jenks nodded and tipped his hat as he climbed out of the car to stretch his long legs.

"How long have you had the car?" Adele asked.

"Only for a few months, it used to belong to my uncle, he purchased it in 1914. It's been well looked after. Ordinarily, I'd have driven here myself but as I'm expecting the wine to be free flowing at the reception, then I thought it best to employ a chauffeur. Jenks has worked for my father for years. He's his butler really, but now doubles up as a chauffeur. Does your father have a car, Adele?"

"Oh, yes, he finally landed in the twentieth century and bought himself a car. I was quite surprised. Oliver never had one. He drove my father's when we went on honeymoon, though," she paused as she chewed on her bottom lip as a painful memory seared her heart. "Quite why he never wanted one, I don't know. He was a careful driver. Very capable." She began to fill up. "Though that could have been as he'd been frittering away our money on that young man, so couldn't afford one."

"Oh come here, old bean," James said, hugging her to his chest as the driver tactfully pretended to check the wheels of the car. "Let it go, Adele, you've been far too brave."

Presently, people began to arrive and soon they were seated inside the small church with its white washed walls and wooden benches. It was very basic really but looked beautiful inside with several floral tributes and altar candles lit as the vicar stood at the pulpit, waiting for the bride to arrive. Donald was seated at the front with his best man. He wasn't in uniform any longer as he'd been demobbed now that the war was over. Instead, he wore a navy suit with a red rose fastened to his lapel as he waited for his bride, Morag, to walk down the aisle.

The bridal march started up as the organist played and Morag, a vision in white organza and lace, walked down the aisle on the arm of one of the doctors who Adele recognised from the hospital at Netley. It was then Adele realised it was too far for Morag's elderly parents to come all the way from Scotland. Really, there was no family here for her just a few close friends and colleagues from the hospital and the same was true for Donald too.

"Dearly beloved..." the vicar began, "we are gathered here today for the wedding of Morag Stewart to Donald Richardson..."

Adele took in every word as it reminded her of her own vows, which although fairly recent, now seemed so long ago. Where did it all go wrong for them both? As if realising how she felt, James gently squeezed Adele's hand as if in reassurance, which was a big help to her as it prevented her from breaking down. There was a prayer and a couple of hymns were sang by the congregation which included, *Love Divine, All Loves Excelling* and *Amazing Grace*, which brought a lump to Adele's throat. Though she longed to flee the church and cry her heart out somewhere on that mountain between the moss and the heather, she stood steadfast with James by her side. Beside him she felt safe and secure, she stole a glance and her heart fluttered madly as she studied his strong jaw line. His dark hair although nicely cut, curled slightly near the nape of his neck. He was tall and broad shouldered. Why had she never seen it before? She did love him, always had, but Oliver's strong show of affection when she returned to Britain from France, had confused her. The French man she'd met during the week had been good company and just what she needed to lift her spirits, but James was solid, strong and firm and she just knew he'd be her rock, if only she'd allow him to be. Up until now she'd done nothing but push him away from her.

As if realising he was being watched, he turned to face her and took her hand in his and smiled. What happened next would be down to her.

***

Following the reception, which was held at a church hall in the small village, James spotted an inn nearby. "I have an idea," he said to Adele, breaking her train of thoughts. She'd been watching Donald and Morag dancing to the first song of the afternoon, which was being played by a lady on a old upright piano in the corner of the hall. The song was, *If You Were the Only Girl in the World*. It was a song that had become popular after It was written for a musical called *The Bing Boys Are Here* that appeared in Leicester Square in London, at the Alhambra Theatre, and Adele adored it. James leant in close to her, close enough that his breath ruffled her hair. How do you fancy staying the night?

Slightly irritated, as she had been deeply absorbed in watching the couple glide around the floor, she turned and said abruptly, "How on earth can we stop over at a church hall?"

He chuckled. "Not here, dear thing. I meant in that inn down the road. That way we wouldn't have to rush back to London. I'll cough up for the driver to stay too. It shall be all very proper, separate rooms and all that."

"Oh," she realised she'd been a little churlish, and although her cheeks suffused with heat, she found herself smiling and agreeing to his suggestion. After all, where was the harm?

"Great, then I shall just pop out of here for a moment and head over there to make the reservations in case others have the same idea, there's snow forecast tonight."

She nodded and watched him leave the hall, he was easily the most handsome man there, though no doubt Morag would hardly agree with that suggestion, she only had eyes for Donald, who seemed to be free of his earlier shell-shocked state. Morag had explained that although he'd been forced to return to duty that night when he was marched out of the hospital in France, he'd later returned to it, and this time, his superior officers seemed more sympathetic. By the time he would have been due to return to the trenches, the war was already over, he'd had a lucky escape. Adele wondered what happened to the other four soldiers who were taken hostage by their superiors that night. She had toyed with asking him but didn't want to cause him any painful memories, particularly now on the day of his wedding.

When the song was over and other couples took to the dance floor, Morag came over to Adele's table. "Where has James gone to?" she asked.

"He's just popped to that little inn down the road to make a couple of reservations, there's bad weather expected later. We've both got some leave due from the hospital too and we thought instead of having to leave early to get back to London, we'd stop the night."

"Oh?" said Morag.

"Look, I'll have none of that..." Adele laughed. "It's not what you think. Besides, I'm still a married woman."

"I knew you'd split up after you'd written to me, Adele..." she lowered her voice, "but I never discovered why."

"It's a long story, but to be honest the age gap was an issue." It was only partly the truth but she couldn't tell Morag the full version, only Belinda and James knew that.

"So what will you do now?"

"Stay and finish my training, I suppose. I might even try to get the

146

wedding annulled as it was never really consummated in the first place."

Her friend draped an arm around Adele's shoulder. "I'm sorry to hear that," she whispered. Then she kissed Adele on the cheek and excused herself to leave so she could mingle with guests. It really was a lovely atmosphere, just the tonic Adele needed.

Ten minutes later, James appeared at her side, "It's all sorted," he explained. "I've made the overnight reservations and we can book in anytime we wish, it's a quiet country inn. Nothing at all like the pubs in London," he chuckled. "Only thing is I've had to book us in as Mr and Mrs as there were only two rooms left over, one for Jenks and the other larger one for us. But if you wish I can bunk up with the chauffeur!" He joked.

"There'll be no need for that, James, we can share," she said quite calmly. Whatever would be would be...

By the time the wedding was over and everyone stood outside the village hall throwing rice as they watched the newly-weds depart in an old car Donald had borrowed from someone, James drew Adele to him. No one there except for the married couple themselves knew who they were, so they could be free and affectionate with one another. "Please, Adele," James said softly, "I never got to kiss you properly in France...We were on the verge of something good together, but you told me to wait as it was neither the time nor the place, and you were absolutely right."

A lump rose in her throat as he drew her toward him and lowering his head, kissed her softly on her lips. He was gentle at first, then his kisses became more passionate and urgent and she knew without a shadow of a doubt when they arrived at the pub, they would make love with one another.

The driver was quite happy having a drink at the bar downstairs whilst James and Adele made an excuse about going to bed. By that time, it was getting quite late, so they wouldn't have looked out of place as they climbed the stairs.

As soon as they entered the room, James took her in his arms and began where he had earlier left off. Gently, he tilted her head back and claimed her mouth with his. Beneath him, her heart pounded for her body to be consumed by him. No man had ever captured her mind or her body before. He swept her up in his arms and took her to the bed all the while saying, "Sshh...It's what we both need and want and we've waited since France for this moment..."

She nodded and allowed him to undress her as she stood trembling, her silk dress slipping to the floor, she stepped out of it leaving her in a pair of cami-knickers, chemise and sheer stockings. James let out a low guttural tone as he pinioned her onto the bed, then removed all his clothing except for his underpants, to lie beside her.

"I'm frightened, James," she whispered.

"There's no need to be when you're with me. You're safe here, Adele. This is not a one-night thing for either of us and we're both consenting adults."

She nodded, and then as if in a hypnotic state, succumbed to his urgent kisses and caresses and before she knew it, her body was ready to allow him entry. It hurt a little as she was a virgin, though not as much as she imagined as she wanted him so badly. She took a few deep breaths in and out and went with the flow, tears were streaming down her face as she realised this was what being a woman felt like. It was so good to be desired and James's face showed a desire that her husband's never had. As he entered her again and again, gently at first and then with great passion all the while checking she was all right, as he'd realised he was her first real lover, everything began to make sense. The tears kept coming and she realised a lot of pent up tension was for everything that had gone on, the battles overseas, the death of her beloved grandfather and her husband's betrayal. Finally, she felt liberated. Not just free, but cleansed in a strange sort of sense. Reborn and rejuvenated.

James's breathing became short and rapid, and finally, she realised he'd reached his release and she clung on to him, drawing his lips towards hers. She loved him so very much.

***

The following morning, she woke early, a bright light filtered in through the bedroom curtains, she looked at the sleeping man beside her and her heart filled with a love she hadn't realised it possible to feel. Without waking him she went to the window and drew a breath to see all was white outside, it had snowed overnight. Naked, she tip-toed to an armchair that was beside the bed, where she had left her clothing. The inn had a shared bathroom so she hoped it was free. After dressing, she slipped across the landing, delighted to find it unoccupied and there she used the lavatory and noticed there was a bath which had hot and cold taps. Not that many places had hot running water but this inn, which was well kept, did. Adele realised that James must have paid a pretty penny for them to stop here with all this luxury.

She quickly filled the bath and washed herself all over. Fresh tablets of soap and clean towels for guests were provided, on a wooden table, the owner had even filled the room with vases of flowers which Adele felt was a lovely touch. She did not have any clean clothes with her, as of course she didn't realise they'd be staying the night, but thankfully, yesterday's clothing looked presentable and suitable to wear at the inn. It was warm enough inside but was probably really cold outside after the snow fall. She'd brought along a knitted cardigan to keep her warm on the journey so wore that over the dress instead of the organza wrap.

Arriving back at the room, freshened up to face the world, she could see that James had woken up and was now sitting up in bed. "Well good morning, Adele," he said cheerfully, yawning and then stretching his arms above his head.

"Good morning," she didn't know why but she felt slightly shy, maybe it was the fact he'd known every inch of her body last night.

He patted his side of the bed, "Come and sit here, will you?" She sat beside him and he kissed her with deep affection. "I'll get washed and dressed and we'll go for breakfast soon."

She nodded. "That would be nice. It snowed overnight."

"Oh? I suppose that will mean we are stranded here..." he chuckled. "I can think of no other better thing in this world than to be with you, Adele."

There was nothing to rush back for as they both had leave from the hospital—it was almost like being on honeymoon themselves.

"If you go quickly, you'll find the bathroom is currently unoccupied, but I expect the other guests will be up and about shortly. Oh, and there's hot and cold running water here!" she enthused.

He quirked a brow. "But what did you expect, dear Adele? Only the best for my beau!"

He leapt out of bed and pulled on his underclothing, trousers and vest and checking there was no one on the landing to see him in that state, hot footed it to the bathroom. Within ten minutes he was washed and back at their bedroom and was putting on his tie and jacket.

They went downstairs for breakfast, to discover tables had been laid with white tablecloths in the bar area and a roaring fire crackled away, by the side of which was a small fir Christmas tree with twinkling silver and gold coloured ornaments. They were the first down apart from one elderly man in the corner, who nodded at them.

The landlady, who introduced herself to Adele as Mrs Peacock, stood ready to take their orders. "What will you have? I've got eggs, bacon, fried bread, tomatoes and mushrooms on this morning, or you can have scrambled eggs on toast if you wish? Oh and I forgot, I have kippers too. Nice and fresh they are as well."

"What would you like, Adele?" James asked, which was nice as Oliver always ordered for her.

"I think I'll have the full breakfast please, Mrs Peacock."

The woman smiled and nodded. "And for you, Mr. Bellingham?"

"The same please and could we have a pot of tea for two?"

She nodded. "Of course, Mr. and Mrs Bellingham."

Adele almost burst out laughing. Of course, James had booked them in as a married couple, she quickly hid her left hand under the table not for Mrs Peacock to notice they weren't wed.

When she had left for the kitchen, James said, "I wouldn't worry about a lack of a wedding ring if I were you, you can always say you lost it."

"Oh, I'm a dreadful liar, James," she smiled.

"In any case, your finger won't be without a ring for long, as soon as your marriage is annulled, I am going to marry you, if you will have me, Adele?"

Could this trip away turn out any more perfect than it already was? "Yes, James, I will," she replied without hesitation, her heart swelling with love for him. Maybe she'd loved him from the very first day she'd answered his question in the operating theatre at the hospital. She'd been surprised that he'd seemed impressed with her when she was a mere student.

Mrs Peacock popped back to the table and handed James a newspaper. "This morning's edition, Mr. Bellingham," she said. "I find most men like a read before their breakfast arrives. And you Madame, I have a copy of 'The Lady' here for you."

Adele wondered if it was a delaying tactic on Mrs Peacock's behalf so that people didn't mind waiting for their breakfasts. It was a nice touch, though.

As they leafed through their reading material, Adele glanced across at James, and gasped when she saw one headline at the bottom of the front page of the newspaper he was reading. It was only a small headline, but it chilled her to the bone. LONDON DOCTOR FOUND HANGED.

"James, look at that article at the bottom of the front page!" she exclaimed. "Is it about Oliver?"

He turned the paper over and read, "The body of a London doctor was discovered at his home yesterday morning. He was found by a servant who had noticed he hadn't risen for breakfast and was shocked when she walked into his bed chamber to find him...h...hanging..." his voice drifted away.

"Oh, it must be him," Adele cried. "He was so distressed and I only went to see him once after I'd left him."

"Now, hold your horses a moment," James said, "we don't know for sure. It gives no details of who this man is and no address either."

"But what can we do? We can't get back to London."

"I'll ask if the landlady knows where I can find a telephone and I'll ring the hospital to find out."

"Good idea."

Mrs Peacock arrived with their breakfasts on a tray, which looked very appetising, but until Adele knew for sure whether the article was about Oliver or not, she would have a hard time forcing down any food.

"Thank you, Mrs Peacock," James said. "You wouldn't know if there's a phone somewhere in the village, would you?"

"There's one at a hotel a few miles from here, but we've recently had our own installed for private business."

Adele's heart sank, maybe the woman wouldn't allow them to use it.

"My word, those breakfasts smell wonderful..." James was buttering the woman up, Adele could tell. "If you would please allow me to use your telephone I need to ring the hospital, I'm a doctor you see, we both are..." James added.

Immediately, Mrs Peacock's haughty manner had changed at the mention of the word, 'doctor'. "Why didn't you say so, of course you may and at no cost to you, Doctor Bellingham."

"If you could just keep both breakfasts warm for us for a few minutes, we shan't be long, we have important business to attend to.

Mrs Peacock nodded and took the plates away and then returned to show them to her parlour where the telephone took pride of place near the window on a small trestle table.

After several attempts of trying to get through to the hospital, James finally got to speak to Woodrow-Smythe, who had seemed bemused that Oliver might have killed himself. "No, he's fine, he's on duty today actually," he related to James.

After James returned the telephone receiver to its stand, he turned to Adele, "There we are, he's fine, he's even on duty today, so he's getting back to normal. Now let's go and eat that scrumptious breakfast!"

Adele smiled, relieved all was well. For a moment there her heart had been in her mouth. It wasn't a nice feeling at all, and although Oliver had betrayed her trust, she was still fond of him and had sympathy for his plight.

When she returned with their breakfasts, James handed Mrs Peacock a couple of sovereigns for her trouble. At last, they could now both relax knowing that Oliver was safe and well. The chauffeur appeared at their table when they were half way through breakfast.

"Sorry to bother you, Sir," he said, addressing James with his cap in hand, "but the roads look impassable at the moment, we could be here for a couple of days."

"Do you have any pressing business for my father?" James asked the man.

"No, Sir."

"Then don't worry about it, we can stay here another night or two. Mrs Peacock is a good cook, there's a bar too, a snooker table with other games I'm informed in another room, a wireless and plenty of books to read. Take it as a well-earned rest from me. Tell Mrs Peacock if you order any drinks, they're all on me."

The chauffeur's eyes lit up as he nodded enthusiastically. "Very well, Sir."

"Sit down and take some breakfast, Mrs Peacock dishes up a lovely full English breakfast."

Wide-eyed, the chauffeur took the single table next door to them.

James leaned over to Adele and whispered, "The poor blighter has a nagging wife and a houseful of kids, this is a luxury for him and a well-earned rest."

Adele patted her lips with her serviette and smiled.

"I think," said James, "we'll order another pot of tea, then afterwards if the Peacocks can loan us some boots and warm clothing, we'll go for a walk in the snow."

How romantic, Adele thought to herself.

***

In the event it was another couple of days before the snow cleared enough for them to return to London, the break had done Adele the power of good and brought her close to James. Following the award ceremony where they were awarded the 'British War Medal' which was a proud moment for them both, they took tea in a Lyons Tea House with Adele's brother, Tom, and James's sister, Arabella. It was good for Adele to see Tom again as she hadn't seen him since the wedding and had some explaining to do. Adele just put it down to incompatibility without any mention of her husband's homosexuality.

Afterwards, when they said goodbye to Tom and Arabella, Adele and James were just rounding the corner on the way back to Mrs Gibson's lodging house when Adele was taken up with a start.

"What's the matter, Adele?" James asked, with a look of concern on his face. "You look like you've seen a ghost!"

"I think I just have...It's that man over there!" she pointed across the street where a young man was walking in the opposite direction. "It's B...Bernhardt!" she exclaimed.

James straightened. "You must be mistaken Adele, surely? That woman, Gilda, who lived with him, said he had drowned in the Thames..."

"Quick!" Adele shouted, "Go after him James, we need to find out."

James turned on his heel and darted off up the street in the same direction the man had taken, it took a while to catch up with him as he was quite physically fit, he finally managed it. By the time Adele reached the pair they were in a heated discussion and she could see it was Bernhardt himself.

"He's just told me that he did go missing but he wasn't dead," James explained.

"That much is obvious!" Adele said fiercely, pointing a finger at him. "Do you know Oliver's really upset as he believes you threw yourself in the Thames."

Bernhardt stood there blankly, shaking his head. "I honestly have no idea why Gilda would say such a thing."

"And that's not all," Adele said angrily, almost spitting out her words, "your so-called friends turned on Oliver when he went to find you, rocking his coach so that he fell and hit his head badly."

The colour now drained from Bernhardt's face.

"Look," James butted in, "it's all over now between Adele and Oliver..."

Adele let out a long breath. "If he means anything to you at all and you really did not know any of this, then go to see him, he's pining for you."

Bernhardt stared at Adele in disbelief. "I can't believe it," he said.

"It's true," she said, without a hint of sadness in her voice. "I left him some time ago, and I shall be annulling the marriage. But all I ask is if you go to him, tell him you have my blessing, but please be discreet as he has his career to think of."

"Oh, I shall!" Bernhardt exclaimed, his face breaking into a huge grin. He tipped his hat off to them both and changed his direction, maybe to visit Oliver.

"Well, you've made someone's day, Adele," James said sagely.

Although she realised that, she hoped all would go well for the pair, she genuinely wanted the best for Oliver. He couldn't change who he was and she would always care for him, so would James.

***

A week later, Adele found herself seated in a solicitor's office, filing for an annulment of her marriage to Oliver. The solicitor said she had good grounds to do so as her marriage was known as a 'voidable marriage', which was a legal marriage that could be cancelled at the option of one of the parties and would be subject to cancellation if contested in court. She could petition to the court for a decree of nullity to declare her marriage void on the grounds that the marriage had not been consummated due to the incapacity of either of them to consummate it.

This made Adele so happy. It would be a way to put the past behind them, and hopefully, would be quicker than petitioning for a divorce. She was going to have to explain things to her parents as best as she could. Deciding not to mention anything about James to them as yet, she left for Wales for a long weekend to spend with them after first sending them a telegram, so they knew to expect her.

***

Doctor Owen picked his daughter up from the railway station in his gleaming car.

"Well, there's great to see you, Adele!" He said, as he hugged her and loaded her luggage onto the back seat. "Oh, and congratulations on your recent award!" He smiled broadly.

"Thank you, Father. I didn't particularly feel deserving of it at the time, but now in retrospect, I suppose I did help a little."

"Help a little? You did more than that my girl, you saved lives. The whole village of Abercanaid has been talking about you and there was a piece about it in the local newspaper. I wasn't supposed to tell you as your mother gave them a photograph of you to go with the article."

"Oh, I hope it was a good one!" She laughed.

"Yes, I think you'll approve. Anyhow, we kept the newspaper for you to see. Actually, your mother purchased several copies to give to friends and family, she's that proud of you." He looked around as if expecting someone else, the train had already begun to move out of the station, blowing up huge clouds of steam. "Oliver not with you then?"

"Er, no." She felt her cheeks heat up. "I've something to tell you both though I'd rather wait until we get back to the house..."

"Is it something we need to tell your mother or should we, how shall I say, 'soften the blow' first?"

Adele's father had a habit of trying to wrap her mother in cotton wool, but on this occasion, Adele felt that maybe her mother didn't need to know the full truth. "Yes, maybe we should speak first and then you decide whether or not to tell her the full story as I understand her health has been delicate of late."

"Hop in the car then, Adele, we'll speak in here before I drive us back, it shall be quite private."

She clambered into the car and seated herself on the leather upholstery beside her father. After a moment's hesitation, she said, "I'm going to get right to the point," she held a breath, then let it out again, "after being married for a few months, I noticed my husband's absences from the home most evenings. After a while, I decided to follow him and discovered he was living a homosexual lifestyle..."

Her father groaned, indicating he felt uncomfortable with the subject matter, but she did not, so carried on, "He admitted it to me and I left him in the end. I tried to work at things, but I don't believe these things can be cured and feel very sorry for him. He is who he is and should be allowed to live as he chooses."

"Sorry for him?" her father spat out the words. "Why on earth would you feel sorry for a man like that, Adele? To think we made him welcome in our home."

"Please don't get angry, Father, it won't solve a thing. To cut a long story short, the marriage was never consummated. I have since begun a relationship with another doctor."

Her father removed his head from his hands. "Who?"

"The surgeon I worked with in Ypres, James Bellingham. You remember me telling you about him?"

Her father brightened momentarily. "Yes, I do. A fine surgeon by all accounts. But how did this happen so fast, Adele?"

"Well, it didn't really. We had feelings for one another in France when we moved to the château hospital to work, but to be honest, I dismissed those even though James wanted me to wait for his return to England. Anyhow, once I was back in London, Oliver made it plain to me, he was in love with me and wanted us to marry."

"No doubt looking for a cover as a married man to camouflage his activities!" Her father scoffed.

"No, I don't believe it was like that, Father. He did have genuine feelings for me, I know he did, but he couldn't turn his back on his sexuality. He's not a bad man, please don't be angry with him."

After a long pause, her father said, "Very well. But you don't tell your mother any of this. Can you divorce?"

"I've been to see a solicitor and it's easier than that, I can get an annulment within a couple of months."

"A good thing too. What will you tell your mother then?"

"Most of the truth, that we weren't compatible. I'm sure you'll both warm to James once you meet him."

"I'm sure I shall." Her father cleared his throat and started up the engine.

***

It was easier for Adele to tell her mother than she imagined. "I have to admit Adele, I did have reservations about you marrying Oliver," she said, when she'd heard the news. "It wasn't just that he was so much older than you as there's a fair age gap between me and your father, it's more of a gut feeling, which I dismissed. Now you say you've met someone else, please tell us all about him?"

Her mother beamed when Adele told her of her work in Ypres with the eminent surgeon, James Bellingham. It was then she realised all was going to be well and they could enjoy a nice pre-Christmas get together. She'd brought presents with her from London and now wished she'd brought James along too, but she hadn't known what sort of reception he'd have received from her parents. She left a couple of days later with an invitation for her to bring James with her for the Christmas festivities. They didn't have a lot of time to spend, but they could fit in a few days between Christmas and the New Year.

***

Easter Monday, April 21st, 1919

The bells chimed out from the quaint little church just down the road from Mrs Gibson's lodging house, for the wedding of Adele to James Bellingham. Adele had decided she didn't want to marry in Merthyr again as there were too many memories there for her to contend with. With time, the bad memory of her marriage to Oliver was beginning to fade and he seemed happier in himself now he and Bernhardt were reunited, but they were keeping their relationship very private, society as it was, wouldn't accept them as a couple. Oliver moved Bernhard into a small apartment, close by to his home, so the young man could escape the clutches of Whitechapel and the dubious folk he'd once mixed with. He was now a commissioned artist for the wealthy folk of Kensington and Chelsea. Adele had toyed with inviting them both to the wedding, but in the end, she thought it best not to, even though she and James were on good terms with both, and to be fair, the pair understood.

Adele's parents attended the wedding, along with her brother, Tommy, and other older siblings. Belinda put aside her Suffragette duties for once to perform the duty of bridesmaid to Adele. Something Adele thought went a little against her preaching, so she was beginning to wonder if her interest in the Suffragette Movement was waning, though she admired her friend's previous passion towards the cause.

Something else she noticed at the wedding was how friendly Belinda and Tommy were with one another, they'd already met previously and got along just fine, which made Adele wonder if there was a relationship in the offing there. Morag and Donald came along to the wedding too, Morag now pregnant with their first child, looking as though she were in full bloom and Donald very attentive towards his new wife.

The wedding was a small affair, the only other people present being, Mrs Gibson and a handful of doctors and nurses from the hospital.

When the wedding service was over, Adele tossed her bridal bouquet over her shoulder and chuckled when she saw it was her brother, Tommy, who'd caught it.

As Adele stood beside James and the wedding guests showered them with rice, she realised she had all she ever wanted. A man she knew she could rely on who would be her rock through both good times and bad, a family who loved her dearly, and good friends. The only thing missing to make her life complete would be to start a family, which she hoped would be sooner rather than later. It was what they both wished for.

It should have been the war to end all wars, but it had taken a savage loss of life. She stopped a moment and taking a red poppy from the bouquet Tommy had handed to Belinda, placed it in Tommy's button hole. The tears in his eyes told her all she needed to know. James understood too. They had all seen things no man nor woman should in their lifetime.

"Lest we forget..." she whispered to James.

"I don't think we ever will," he replied, giving her hand a gentle squeeze of reassurance as they went off to make a new life together.

The End

Seasons of Change Series

1. Black Diamonds
2. White Roses
3. Blue Skies
4. Red Poppies

These titles and others are available from Amazon